Hamfist Down!

Evasion, Survival and Combat in the Jungle

By

G. E. Nolly

www.GENolly.com

www.HamfistAdventures.com

This book is a work of fiction. Names, characters, places and incidents are either the product of the author's imagination or are used fictionally. Any resemblance to actual persons, living or dead, or to actual events or locales is entirely coincidental.

Version 2012.04.22

ISBN 978-0-9754362-2-6

This book is dedicated to American military veterans, past, present, and future.

1

August 1, 1969

Getting shot down sucks. Bailing out after getting shot down is worse. If you're shot down and you get killed, your fight is over. If you're shot down and bail out, your fight is just beginning. And bailing out over Laos is about as bad as it can get.

A few months earlier, I'd had lunch with a Green Beret Lieutenant, nicknamed Snake, who was doing some Special Ops work, called Prairie Fire, with our squadron. I had worked with him on a few occasions, flying him over the area of operations to find areas he thought would make good LZs – landing zones.

His job was to lead six-member teams, three Americans and three indigenous, into Laos to try to search for aircrew members who had been shot down. The team would be air-lifted to the selected LZ by army helicopters, and they used Covey FACs to help with air support if they got into trouble. And they frequently made contact with the enemy and needed air support.

Since the gomers could hear the chopper when it was inbound to the LZ, it was pretty hard for the team to stay hidden. One way to confuse the gomers was to perform the team insertion – the infil – with one chopper, and at the same time have six or seven other choppers land at decoy LZs. The choppers would land, wait a few seconds, then lift off and leave. Just like a real infil. So the gomers never would know if the LZ was a real infil or a decoy. The team would do the extraction – the exfil – the same way.

Every now and then the team would find a live crewmember, and call for an immediate exfil. Most of the time, though, they would find the crewmember's remains.

Snake was a tough-as-nails combat veteran on his third tour. I'd taken him up on a few flights to look for candidate LZ sites, and he was absolutely fearless. When we'd get shot at with triple-A, he was as cool as a cucumber. I'd be jinking and maneuvering like crazy, and he'd be sitting in the observer seat looking totally unconcerned. You'd think he was watching television.

But when he would talk about finding the

bodies of pilots in Laos, he would really get emotional. His eyes would well up.

"I've seen a lot, Hamfist, but I've never seen anything like what the Pathet Lao does to the guys they catch," he said, "You know, we go to the base theater to watch a movie for entertainment. These bastards torture their prisoners for entertainment. That's their evening movie. One of the pilots we found," he paused and wiped his eyes, "had his hands cut off and he'd been skinned."

"On one mission a few months ago, we were outside a small village, avoiding contact, just recon. I had a good view of a few huts, and I suddenly heard the loud yelping of a dog that was obviously in a lot of pain. I looked with my binocs in the direction of the howling, and saw a Laotian woman, probably in her sixties, casually bending back the leg of a small dog. Suddenly, the leg snapped, and the dog howled even louder."

"These people actually think that if the dog suffers before they kill it," Snake continued, "the meat will taste better. For all I know, it might, but you can see that these bastards have no compassion."

"I'll tell you one thing," he concluded, "I'll never let them get me alive. The Raven FACs carry poison pills with them, shellfish toxin, to use if they get caught. I tried to get something like that, but I couldn't get any." He reached down into a small leather loop sewn inside the back of his boot and pulled out a .45 caliber cartridge. "This one's for me. If I'm ever out of ammo and about to get captured, I'm using this one on myself."

I didn't carry a .45 caliber Model 1911 like Snake. The Air Force service firearm was the .38 Special, a six-shot revolver, and at DaNang we were issued six rounds plus six tracer bullets, ostensibly for signaling at night. Twelve bullets. That was it. After my conversation with Snake, I decided that if I was ever shot down and had to use my pistol, I would only fire at the enemy eleven times. I would save that last round for myself.

2

August 1, 1969

I didn't have any sense of falling, and I had no idea which way was up, or how high above the jungle I was. I initially hesitated, and really considered not pulling my parachute D-ring. End it quick.

Then, like watching a movie in fast-forward, I pictured an Air Force staff car pulling up to my mom's house in Pensacola. There would be a field-grade officer, probably a Colonel. And a Chaplain. And my mom's worst nightmare would come true. She would become a Gold Star Mother.

My Aunt Rosalie was a Gold Star Mother. Her son Johnnie, my cousin, had been killed on Omaha Beach on D-Day. Aunt Rosalie never got over it. I was always uncomfortable visiting her house, because it was a shrine to Johnnie.

Aunt Rosalie was frozen in time. When I was a kid, we visited her about once a month. Her house was always dark, and there was a clock on the mantle that made a loud ticking sound that seemed to dominate the room whenever there was a pause in the conversation, which was often. The photo of Johnnie in his uniform, probably taken during basic training, was illuminated by a spotlight in the ceiling that always remained on. There was a black ribbon around the frame. His face in the picture, it seemed to me, had a look like he knew he was going to die.

There was another picture on the mantle, of Aunt Rosalie and Uncle Sam with Johnnie, taken at his high school graduation, probably just a month or two before he enlisted. Aunt Rosalie and Uncle Sam looked so slim and vibrant in the photo. Now, Uncle Sam was no longer around – he had died from a heart attack when I was just a young kid – and Aunt Rosalie was at least a hundred pounds overweight. When she would reach out to hug me, the fat on the bottom of her arms would flap like a butterfly's wings.

Every time we would visit, every time, Aunt Rosalie would find a reason to bring out Johnnie's final letter, written on June 5th, 1944. Aunt Rosalie would always hold the letter with trembling hands, and start reading in a soft voice.

"Dear Mom and Dad,

By the time you receive this letter you'll have heard about the special mission I'm about to go on..."

Every time she read the letter, at this exact point, her voice would trail off, and she would read the rest of the letter silently, her lips moving, silent tears streaming down her face.

Cousin Johnnie had died before I was even born, and Aunt Rosalie's world still revolved around Johnnie. I didn't want my Mom to be like that.

And then I pictured Samantha. How would she even find out about me? She was in Tokyo, and, as far as the Air Force was concerned, she didn't even exist.

Visualizing this took, at most, a second or two.

Fuck it. I wouldn't be giving up that easily. Like Sergeant McCoy had said back at Clark, "Never give up. Make them *earn* you." I reached for my parachute D-ring, found it, and gave a mighty pull.

My chute opened with a jolt so hard my helmet came off and fell into the darkness. Off to my left I saw what was left of my airplane, wildly spinning and trailing flames. It continued spinning, and then was swallowed by the triple-canopy jungle about a hundred meters from me, with a loud explosion.

I swung a few times, and then immediately felt myself crashing into the trees. I crossed my arms in front of my face, crossed my legs, tightened my body the best I could, and waited to come to rest.

The sound of breaking tree limbs immediately triggered a cacophony of jungle sounds. Birds, monkeys, and other unknown animals made loud, screeching sounds to warn of an invader.

And then the area near me was silent. I found myself hanging from my parachute straps in total darkness. The lack of illumination, and the quiet, were actually strangely comforting. The same animal sounds that had registered alarm when I had invaded their sanctuary would warn me of any approaching enemy soldiers. Off in the distance, perhaps a half mile away, I could hear the sound of trucks.

I had no idea how high up in the trees I was, and it would have been foolish to attempt to lower myself with my Personnel Lowering Device – PLD – in the blackness. I decided that all I could do was wait until daylight, and try to get rescued.

I was fairly certain that my parachute had been swallowed up by the jungle, and would be invisible from the air. And it was highly unlikely that there would be any attempted SAR before daylight. Especially after the experience of Jolly 22 and his Spads when they worked that night SAR several months ago. I was fairly certain that the fighters I was working, Gunfighter 33 flight, would have reported me going down, and would have contacted King, the Rescue Coordination Center.

I listened intently. From the silence, I was pretty sure there were no gomers nearby. I had to pee in the worst way. I cautiously unzipped my flight suit from the bottom and relieved myself. Still no sounds below.

Far, far above, I could hear some aircraft. They sounded like F-4s. Probably Gunfighter 33. I felt around in the pockets of my survival vest until I found my URC-64 transceiver. I extended the antenna to turn it on, turned the volume knob as low as it would go, and held the microphone part of the radio up against my lips. I whispered into the microphone.

"Mayday, mayday, mayday. This is Covey

218 Alpha, in the blind, on GUARD. I'm hung up in some trees now, and I believe I'm uninjured. I'll try to lower myself and make radio contact at daybreak. Covey 218 Alpha going radio silent."

Up above, I heard an F-4 light his burner momentarily. He had heard me!

My parachute harness was really starting to cut off the circulation to my legs. I tried to shift my weight a bit, but it was no use. I would just have to wait until morning.

This was going to be a long night.

3

August 2, 1969

During the night, I heard an O-2 flying overhead, and I briefly got on my URC-64 about every hour or so to let the Covey know I was still okay. I kept my transmissions short to save battery life. Even though I wasn't continuously talking to the Covey, it was comforting to know he was in the area.

It turned out the first Covey on-scene was my room-mate, Fish. During one of our brief conversations, I said, "You better do a good job of getting me out of here, or you'll end up being my Summary Courts Officer. It's shitty duty."

"Looks like you haven't lost your sense of humor, Hamfist. We'll get you out." Then he paused. "Hey, Hamfist, if we don't get you out, can I have your camera?"

That really lifted my spirits, knowing that we could have a little moment of levity. It was dark, the gomers had no idea where I was, and

I was safe, at least for now.

The mention of the camera got me thinking about the pictures I had taken on R&R in Tokyo, less than a week ago. The film was still in the camera. There had been a few exposures remaining, and I hadn't wanted to develop the film until I had used it all. Suddenly, I felt like an idiot, being such a cheap fuck. As a result, I never even got to see the photos of what was probably the best week of my life. There would be photos of Samantha and me together. Lots of photos. Now the only perosn to see them will be my Summary Courts Officer.

Probably as a way of getting my mind off of my current situation, I thought back of my R&R in Tokyo. Was it really only a few days ago? And was it really only for five days?

I didn't think you could fall in love with someone in such a short time, but I was sure I was in love with Sam.

On my third day in Tokyo, we got all dressed up again.

"I have someplace special to take you," she said.

We got in the limo, she said something in Japanese to the driver, and we drove for about 20 minutes, ending up at a building with a garish sign that proclaimed it to be the Nichigeki Music Hall. As we entered, there was a prominent sign that read, "No photography allowed".

An usher escorted us to our seats in a theater with a large stage. A small placard in front of each seat read, "When taking pictures, not to use flash". Inscrutable, these Japanese!

Then the show started. There was a chorus line of about thirty girls, all about our age, totally topless, wearing g-string bottoms. To be honest, I can't remember what the hell the show was about. I remember there were some water effects, and a lot of dancing. I was mesmerized by all those tits!

In my peripheral vision, I could see Sam occasionally glancing over at me, and I tried to act nonchalant. I don't think I did a very good job.

After the show, we hailed a cab.

"Did you like the show?" she asked.

"Actually, I did. I've never seen that many breasts at one time."

"Me neither, not even in the locker room in college."

"I had heard that Japanese girls were all flat-chested. They sure didn't look that way, and you..." I caught myself before saying anything else. I had felt so close to Sam that I thought I could say anything, but I was afraid that I might have ventured too far. She didn't seem concerned.

"That was probably true, before the war. Now the diet in Japan is much more like the States, and Japanese kids today are much taller than they were a generation ago. And better endowed. It's from better nutrition."

"You saw how small Mommy is," she continued, "about five-one, but I'm five-four. And, you know, Daddy isn't very tall."

"He's the same height as me – five-nine."

"What I meant is, he's the perfect height," she replied, squeezing my arm.

I instinctively flexed my arm when she grabbed it.

"Wow, you're really hard," she remarked.

"Of course I am, after that show we just saw."

Sam put her hand up to cover her mouth as she laughed.

"God, I wish we had met back when we were in college," she said.

"Me too," I replied, "We have some lost time to make up for."

14

I shot a quick glance at her chest, and she caught me.

"I'm sorry. I didn't mean to stare."

"No problem. I understand, you've been away at war. I'll answer the question you're too shy to ask: 36C."

I couldn't think of anything clever to say, and we sat in silence for the 15-minute ride to Roppongi. This time we went to a newly-opened place, the Club Mugen.

The music was great, a lot more slow songs than the place we had gone to a few days earlier. When we danced to "Strangers In The Night", we held each other tightly, and I didn't want the song to end. When Sam went to the rest room, I went up to the band leader, who was also the lead singer. He was a perfect mimic. When he sang a Johnnie Mathis song, he sounded exactly like Johnny Mathis. When he sang Strangers In The Night, he sounded exactly like Frank Sinatra.

I gave him 1000 yen, and asked him to play Strangers In The Night every fifteen minutes.

He responded, "No speak Engrish".

I was amazed. He sang with absolutely no accent, but couldn't speak a word of English. Pointing at my Rolex, and the 12 o'clock, 3 o'clock, 6 o'clock and 9 o'clock parts of the watch face, I tried to explain what I wanted.

I wasn't sure whether he understood me, but they played it four times an hour while we were there, and Strangers In The Night became our song.

That night seemed so very long ago.

I had a canteen filled with water on my web belt, and I periodically took sips from it. By dawn, it was empty.

Finally, dawn came, and I heard an OV-10 overhead. It was Scooter Scoville. I didn't know Scooter all that well. In fact, I didn't know most of the OV drivers very well, since I was normally asleep when they were flying, and vice-versa. Other than squadron meetings, we O-2 drivers didn't have a whole lot of contact with the OV drivers.

From what I had seen from my few contacts with Scooter, he seemed like a sharp guy. He had arrived at DaNang about a month after me, as a Captain, and had pinned on Major a few months later. He was at the bar the night I had rung the bell and bought drinks for everyone, and later had told me that I was a really fun drunk.

I think he was trying to identify me, to make

sure I wasn't a gomer on the radio.

"Hey, Covey 218 Alpha," he said, "remind me, what was that you did at the club a few months ago?"

"I wore my hat, rang the bell, and yelled dead bug."

"Roger, Covey, we have assets alerted. Let me know when you're out of your present position."

Obviously, it was fruitless to bring assets to rescue me until I was out of the trees.

The sun was now fully up, and I could see my surroundings. I looked down, and still couldn't tell how high I was, because of the foliage below me. Also, it was still pretty dark on the jungle floor because of the triple canopy.

I removed the PLD from my harness, passed the webbing through the V of my parachute risers, and snapped it to the ring on the front of my harness.

As I was attaching the friction device, it occurred to me how fortunate I had been to have received instruction in the use of the PLD at snake school. It would be difficult – no, impossible – for anyone to use the PLD without instruction and practice. I thought of Mitch, and hoped he hadn't been hung up in trees when he got shot down. Being stuck in the trees, either starving or becoming a target for gomers to shoot at, would be a terrible way to die.

I released my parachute risers and lowered myself to the jungle floor. My legs had fallen asleep because of the constriction of my harness, and I collapsed like a sack of potatoes onto the moist jungle floor. I frantically massaged my legs, and finally started to regain feeling. After a few minutes, I was able to stand. The jungle was still quiet.

It was obvious that the PLD hanging down from the tree would alert anyone looking for me where to start their search. Since the PLD stuck out like a sore thumb, I just left my harness there also.

And then I did something really dumb. I took off my web belt, with the canteen, and left it with my harness. I figured I didn't need it, since the canteen was already empty, and it might make some noise flapping against my hip when I moved.

I needed to put some distance between my parachute and myself, and fast. I could still hear the sound of trucks in the distance, so I headed in the opposite direction. I was not on any kind of trail, but it was fairly easy to move through the jungle. That meant it would be easy for anyone to follow me, also. I needed to get to an area of better concealment. I was already sweating profusely.

I remembered that, in survival school, they said we should travel on the "military crest", about two-thirds of the way up any ridge line of travel. This would minimize being silhouetted against the sky.

I looked ahead and to my right, saw a ridge line, and headed toward it. The brush was getting thicker, and I was moving a lot slower. Fortunately, the brush was higher also, so probably the gomers couldn't see me.

Suddenly, I heard automatic weapons fire, a lot of it. It sounded like it came from below me on the hill, near where I had come down, and sounded fairly close. I ducked down under a large bush, and remained perfectly still. I tried to burrow into the ground under the bush, to become one with the jungle. In no time at all I was being attacked by both ants and mosquitos. I didn't dare swat at them or move at all. I slowly moved my hand up to pinch off my nose, so the ants wouldn't get in there. As I breathed through my mouth, ants kept crawling in.

I remembered Sergeant McCoy saying,

"There's more protein in a pound of ants than in a pound of hamburger." I swallowed them as fast as they crawled into my mouth. They didn't have any perceptible taste, and a few felt like they got stuck in my throat. Tenacious little bastards.

The gomers had probably found my parachute harness. Now they knew there was a survivor, and they were trying to flush me out. If I hadn't been told about this tactic at snake school, I probably would have run for my life. That was exactly what the gomers wanted.

In my mind, I could still hear Sergeant McCoy. "Every year, hunters get lost and their bodies don't get found for months, even years. If you don't move, there's almost no way they will find you if you're well hidden. I'll say it again, never give up, make them *earn* you."

I could hear the gomers talking, and finally their voices were getting more distant. I could also hear an aircraft, it sounded like an A-1, overhead. I removed my lensatic compass from the lower pocket of my survival vest and got a bearing on the general direction of the gomers.

Then I took out my URC-64 and made sure the acoustic coupler was firmly attached. The coupler was a plastic disc that fit tightly over the microphone, and had a hollow rubber tube attached. I put the end of the tube in my ear, turned on the URC-64, and lifted the disc to whisper into the mike.

"This is Covey 218 Alpha. I've moved from my original position, and I'm uninjured. There are gomers about 50 meters to my south."

"Okay, Alpha, we hear you loud and clear. First, a little housekeeping. What is your SAR ID number?"

The Search and Rescue – SAR – ID number was a number that we individually chose to put in our SAR file, so the SAR forces could confirm we were who we said we were. I had made the designation in survival school, at Fairchild Air Force Base, almost a year earlier.

"Before any of you decide to be wise-asses," the instructor had said, "I want you to know that there are sixteen POWs in the Hanoi Hilton with ID number 6969. So choose a number you'll remember that will be unique to you." I remembered being proud of myself for choosing such a unique number. And now, for the life of me, literally, I couldn't remember it.

"This is Covey 218 Alpha. Look, I think I have a concussion, and I just can't remember my number."

"Roger, Alpha, stand by one. Spad flight,

button two, go."

"Two."

Shit. I could tell they thought a gomer had gotten hold of my radio. And I didn't blame them. If I couldn't convince them I was who I said I was, I would really be fucked.

"Spad flight, check."

"Two."

"Alpha, this is Spad One. Do you have your KAK wheel with you?"

"I lost it when I bailed out." That much I remembered. I had been using it to authenticate Gunfighter flight right before the missile hit me.

"Okay, Alpha, we're going to have to take a little break here. If you can remember your SAR ID, come back up on Guard and we'll restart the SAR."

I was getting frantic. My head was throbbing, I was dog tired, and I was hungry. Damn it, I wanted to be picked up, and now!

"Listen to me, you shit-eating cocksucker," I whispered into the mike, "you get your sorry ass back here, bring in the mother-fucking Jolly, and get me the fuck out of here."

"Okay, Alpha, spoken like a true GI. Jolly 41 is inbound. First we need to locate you. Do you have a clear view of the sky?"

I carefully poked my head out from under the bush where I'd been hiding. I could see the sky.

"Affirmative."

"Okay, get your mirror ready, and signal me when I fly overhead. Can you hear my aircraft?"

"I hear you. It sounds like you need to come north."

I stayed crouched down and took out my signaling mirror. Then I got on my back and got the spot from the sun to reflect onto my hand. I saw Spad. I aimed the spot from the reflection of the sun by moving my hand toward Spad, then quickly removing my hand and wiggling the mirror.

"I have a tally on you, Alpha."

Suddenly, there was a lot of automatic weapons fire coming from the bottom of the hill.

While the firing was going on, I didn't need to whisper. "Spad, you're taking fire from down the hill."

"Roger, Alpha. I have the area in sight. You'll need to stand by for a little while, so we can neutralize the ground fire before we bring Jolly 41 in."

"Roger."

The Spads started strafing the area where the automatic weapons fire had originated. I could see that it would be a little while before my pickup.

I used the time to inventory the contents of my survival vest and my flight suit pockets.

In no particular order, my vest had:

gyro jet flare gun

condom

six tracer rounds

two day/night flares

camouflage face paint

first aid kit

SDU5/E strobe light with blue filter

signal panel

two ten-ounce cans of water

signaling mirror

survival hunting knife, 6-inch blade

I always got a kick out of the survival instructor telling us the condom was a "water container". Beats the shit out of me what they really had in mind when they put the condom in the kit. I took the camouflage stick and smeared it on my face, using the survival mirror to make sure I didn't miss any part of my pasty-white face.

I emptied all of the pockets of my flight suit, to see if I had any other items that could be useful, and remembered I had the orange switchblade knife in the pecker pocket of my flight suit. The switchblade was a survival knife that was issued to all aircrew members, to be used to cut parachute riser cords if they became entangled. The pecker pocket was a narrow pocket on the front of the upper left leg of the flight suit. It actually looked like you could stick your pecker in it. It was designed to hold the switchblade knife. In snake school, we had practiced retrieving the switchblade from the pecker pocket with our eyes closes.

I had heard a story that a fighter jock had once bailed out, due to flying into a thunderstorm, somewhere in New York, and flagged down some cops to take him into town. When they discovered his switchblade, they arrested him, and he spent the night in jail. As a result of that, we were each issued a card authorizing us to carry a switchblade knife.

I also had some water in the lower leg pockets of my flight suit. The Covey squadron had a large refrigerator in the ready room, and always had a bunch of plastic flasks filled with water in the freezer. Before the flight, as usual, I had grabbed two frozen flasks and put them in my pockets.

I also found two other items I had forgotten were in my lower leg pockets: my *daruma* and my miniature binoculars.

4

August 2, 1969

I had received my *daruma* less than a week before, as a gift from Tom and Miyako, Sam's parents, as I was leaving Tokyo at the end of R&R. The *daruma* was a small doll with a weighted base, that always righted itself when it was tipped over. And it had no eyes painted on its face.

The owner of the *daruma* was supposed to paint one eye on the doll when he set a goal, and then paint the other eye on the *daruma* when the goal was achieved.

When I returned to DaNang from Tokyo, I gave a lot of thought to what goal would be represented by the eye. Once I had made up my mind, I went to the BX and bought a small jar of black paint and a narrow brush from the department that sold model airplane kits. While I was at the BX, I also bought a 45 rpm Frank Sinatra record, with Strangers In The

Night on the A side and Summer Wind on the B side, and airmailed it to Sam. When I got back to my room, I carefully painted an eye on my *daruma*. It was an almond-shaped eye, like Sam's. I thought I did a pretty good job.

On a whim, I had stuffed the *daruma* into my flight suit lower left leg pocket right before leaving for this mission. I thought it might bring me good luck, kind of like pissing on the revetments. Lots of luck it had brought me so far.

The binoculars had been a gift from Sam. She had taken me on a whirlwind tour of Tokyo, and at one point we went to Akihabara, the optics and electronics district. We walked around the stores and did a lot of window shopping.

At one point, I had examined a really neat set of Nikon binoculars. They were very small, opera glasses, really. And they had great resolution. I had thought about buying them, then thought better of it. After all, the Air Force provided us with binoculars to use on our flights. And, to be honest, they were kind of expensive.

Sam had seen me coveting the binoculars, and, at some point, probably when I was in the rest room, had bought them. Right before we got into the limo to go to Yokota Air Base for my return flight to DaNang, she gave them to me.

"Ham, I want you to have something that's really nice, an extravagance. And I hope you'll think of me when you use them."

G. E. Nolly

5

August 2, 1969

The SAR was going to be almost too easy. The Spads and the fighter aircraft spent a lot of time, perhaps an hour or more, working over the enemy. It looked like they had been neutralized. During the strike, I moved up the hill to a more secure location, and advised Spad where I was.

I made visual contact with the Spads, and they surveyed the area and found a good pickup point about 50 meters from my hiding place. There was no enemy reaction at all when they flew over.

I could hear Jolly 41 arriving, and I carefully moved out to the pickup point.

Suddenly, the entire area erupted in massive gunfire. Automatic weapons, AK-47s, ZPU, 23 mike-mike, everything. Jolly took numerous hits, and smoke started billowing from one of it's engines. It limped off out of sight.

I had been used as bait for a flak trap.

The Spads attacked the gun emplacements, but there were too many guns to completely neutralize. One of the Spads took a hit and made a hasty retreat. The other Spad stayed on scene, and Covey 245 directed him, along with some F-4s and A-7s, against more targets.

It seemed like there were two new guns for every gun that was destroyed. It reminded me of the Disney movie of The Sorcerer's Apprentice, where Mickey Mouse would chop the brooms in half, and then there would be twice as many brooms carrying buckets of water.

There was no possible way they could make a rescue with that kind of ground fire.

To make matters worse, low clouds were moving in, and it started to rain.

I was getting pelted by the heavy rain, and thought of what I had seen during a trip to the Freedom Hill BX.

To get to the Freedom Hill BX, we had to travel off base at DaNang. Usually, we just hitched a ride with any available military vehicle heading in the right direction. On one of my trips to the BX, it started raining heavily. As we drove past the shanty town, I saw local gomers squatting down, trying to make themselves smaller targets from the rainstorm. They didn't have anywhere to go to get out of the rain. That was what I now felt like.

During the rainstorm, it seemed like everything was put on hold. There were no airstrikes, no ground fire. Nothing. I knew the rain would mask any sounds of my movement, so I started moving further along the ridge. I made periodic contact with the SAR forces, and kept moving for the next several hours. I was making slow progress.

The rain stopped, but it was now getting dark.

Spad came up on the radio.

"Covey 218 Alpha, you're going to need to relocate for us to be able to get a successful SAR. See if you can get a few miles away before daybreak, and we'll give it another try tomorrow."

I answered, "Roger," and turned off my URC-64 to conserve battery life.

He was right, of course. There was simply no way they could get me out of there. I would need to move. But I knew, and he probably also knew, that moving at night was almost impossible.

I've never felt as alone as I did at that moment. It became clear to me that I was going to die in the next 24 hours. And a great sadness came over me.

I was sad for the life I would never live. I had met my soul-mate, after missing the chance to meet her six years earlier, and now I would never see Sam again.

I wondered if it was going to hurt when my time came. I thought back to when Dad had hypnotized me, when I was a teenager, and I didn't feel any pain, even when he stuck me with a needle. I wondered if I could hypnotize myself so that I wouldn't feel pain.

And I thought of the night Dad died.

It was June 22, 1960. A few days after Father's Day. I was fifteen years old, and probably a real pain in the ass teenager. But, for some reason, Dad and I had never been closer. We did a lot together.

Every night, after he came back from work, we'd go to the small exercise room we had set up in the attic of our house, and we'd lift weights together.

Dad had previously been flying in the Air Guard, but finally retired because Mom worried so much about his flying and being gone so much. He bought a liquor store, and was home every night. I probably saw more of him after he bought that store than I had in all the years leading up to it.

Mom went to the store to pick Dad up at closing time, like she did every night. I changed into my exercise outfit, and waited. They were late coming back. Probably stopped off to pick up ice cream or something.

I heard a car in the driveway, and I put the starting weights on the bar. Dad hated it if I didn't have the weights set up for our first exercise.

The door of our house opened, but it wasn't Dad, wasn't Mom. It was Phil, Dad's war buddy. He called out to me.

"Hamilton."

I knew immediately that something was wrong. And I knew, I swear I knew, that something had happened to Dad. It could have been anything, could have been the road was closed, could have been something happened to Mom, anything. But I knew, for sure, that something had happened to Dad.

Phil's eyes were red.

"Hamilton, have a seat." His lower lip was trembling.

I didn't want to sit down. If I sat down, I would hear the bad news. If I stayed standing, I wouldn't hear it, and it wouldn't be real. Phil looked at me. I sat down.

"There's been an accident."

"What kind of accident?"

"Someone tried to rob the store. Your father's been shot. I'm sorry, Hamilton, he's passed away."

I'd never heard the term "passed away" in person. I knew what it meant, but it didn't register.

"Will he be all right?" I was crying, bawling.

"Hamilton, he died. I'm sorry." Phil was crying also. I think he started crying before I did.

The next three days were a blur. I wish I could have been more alert, to understand what was happening, to mark the moment. Relatives cycled in and out. An uncle went to Dad's workroom and picked up one of Dad's tools.

"I want to keep this as a legacy of your father." I didn't object. I was in a trance.

I wondered if, at that last second, Dad knew he was going to die. Did he have a chance to think of his life, the way I have a chance now?

I'd probably be asking him soon enough. And I'd finally get to meet Cousin Johnnie.

I reached into my pocket and took out my wallet. The only picture in my wallet was the one we had taken on that Father's Day. Mom, Dad and me standing together. In the dim light I could barely make out the image. I returned the photo to my wallet and put my wallet back in my pocket.

The day Dad was killed was the watershed moment of my life story. It was like BC and AD of the Gregorian calendar. There were things that happened before Dad died, and things that happened after Dad died. That was the yardstick I used to mark events in my life. I wondered if that would be the way Sam would measure her life. I hoped not. I hoped she would move on and have a wonderful life with someone who loved her.

As the light dimmed, I had to move slower. I didn't want to end up falling off a cliff or tripping and injuring myself. After a while, I could hear the sound of running water, a small stream. I really needed to refill my water bottles, but I knew from snake school that the gomers would be watching any water supplies to try to flush me out. I dug in under a large bush and waited to see if there were any gomers nearby.

After a few minutes I could hear some people moving nearby. Then I heard the sound of them walking away. I couldn't tell if all of them had walked away, or just a few of them. I continued to wait. I remembered what Sergeant McCoy had said. My goal was to see if I could remain still enough for my self-winding Rolex to stop.

After about two hours I heard someone fart. It came from about ten feet from me. I absolutely froze. I was afraid to even breathe. I could hear my pulse pounding in my temples, and I felt like the gomers could hear it also.

Shortly after the fart, a gomer said something in what sounded like Vietnamese, and another gomer replied. Then I heard a lot of bushes rustling, and I heard the gomers walking away. I waited another two hours, totally still, and there were no more sounds. I had waited out the gomer scouts.

As the light started to increase, I could see the stream about twenty meters from my hiding place. I carefully looked around, then edged over to the stream and refilled my water flasks. I felt like a complete fool for not bringing my canteen.

As soon as I had more water, I moved out,

away from the stream. I moved slowly and carefully, stopping every few steps to listen for any signs of life nearby. By dawn, I estimated that I had moved at least two miles from the original flak trap.

I checked my URC-64 battery level, and it was getting really low. I made a call in the blind, and a Covey answered. It was Fish again. Good old Fish. He *really* didn't want to become a Summary Courts Officer!

I could hear the sound of his engines, and I vectored him over my position. I put the blue lens with the directional snout over my survival strobe light and signaled Fish. He was able to plot my position, and he told me he had called in the SAR forces again.

G. E. Nolly

6

August 3, 1969

As I was waiting for SAR to arrive, I listened carefully to the ambient sounds. In the distance, I could again hear trucks, a lot of trucks. I took out my binoculars to survey the area. I wanted to look around to see if I could determine any threats. I didn't want a replay of yesterday's flak trap. I carefully stuck my head out from behind the bush where I'd been hiding, looked in the direction of the truck sounds, and raised the binoculars to my eyes. I adjusted the focus and swept the area. Then I saw the truck park trans-shipment point.

It was totally hidden from the air due to the trees, but it was a really large truck park. I saw twenty, maybe thirty, vehicles, and several storage sheds. Some of the vehicles had large barrels in the truck beds, probably fuel. I also saw gomers carrying what looked like large, narrow cylinders and placing them into the truck beds. Probably 122 millimeter rockets.

I took out my lensatic compass and got a bearing on the truck park. My guess, based on how small the trucks and the gomers looked, was that they were 300 yards from me. When I had played golf at the Academy Golf Course, I had gotten fairly good at estimating distances based on the appearance of the apparent size of the people in the party ahead of me. I was pretty sure the trucks were 300 yards away.

I hadn't heard an O-2 overhead in a while. I got back on my URC-64. "Do we still have a Covey on site?"

"Affirmative," came the reply, "Covey 234 is holding off to the east."

"Roger, Covey 234. We have a massive truck park and trans-shipment point 300 meters east southeast from my position. If you can put in a willie pete, I can vector you in."

"Covey 234 is in for the mark."

I observed the impact of the white phosphorous rocket. A few seconds later I heard the explosion. I hadn't realized a willie pete made so much noise when it hit.

"Okay Covey 234, if you have assets ready, put them in 40 meters east of your mark."

Covey 234 answered, "I have an F-4 coming in from the north."

The bombs hit near the target, but a bit short.

"Move the next bombs 20 meters north," I transmitted.

"Roger."

The next set of bombs was right on target, and secondary explosions started cooking off, getting more violent with each explosion. I was ecstatic. During the airstrike, I was back to being a FAC. I had forgotten to be scared. I was doing what I had been trained to do.

And, in my excitement, I had forgotten to keep my voice lowered. I suddenly realized I was speaking, sometimes yelling, into the URC-64, and I wasn't sure how long I had been doing that.

At about the same time, I started receiving automatic weapons fire. I could hear the bullets hitting the trees and bushes near me, but I couldn't see who was shooting. I crouched down behind my bush and drew my pistol from the holster on my survival vest. I flipped open the cylinder and checked my ammunition. I had six tracer rounds loaded. I reached down to re-check where I had put the remaining bullets. They were in the bottom right side pocket of my vest.

The automatic weapons fire was getting closer, from down the hill. I peered around the bush and saw four gomers shooting in my direction. They were looking directly at me, and I couldn't believe they were missing me with their fire.

I got on my URC-64. "This is Covey 218 Alpha taking automatic weapons fire from some gomers down the hill. I need support, now."

"We see them, Alpha. But they're too close to you for us to engage. You need to put some distance between them and you. Or you need to take care of them yourself."

Take care of them myself? What the fuck was he talking about? Now I was scared, really scared. My hand was shaking so hard I almost couldn't close the cylinder on my revolver.

7

August 3, 1969

This was it. They were closing in on me, and I had, at most, two or three more minutes to live. And then, a funny thing happened. I stopped being scared. For some reason, I thought of the American Fighting Man's Code of Conduct, and a strange calm came over me.

At the Academy, I had been required to memorize it as part of Doolie Knowledge:

I am an American Fighting Man. I serve in the forces which guard my country and our way of life. I am prepared to give my life in their defense. I will never surrender of my own free will.

It hit me like a ton of bricks. I'm not a fucking quivering evader. I'm an American Fighting Man, goddam it. It was time to take the fight to the enemy.

The gomers firing at me were about twenty meters down the hill. There were four of them.

I just couldn't believe they were firing at me and missing. Then it occurred to me – these gomers weren't soldiers. They were probably just like Nguyen that Jack the FAC had told us about. Probably conscripts, human mules carrying supplies down the Ho Chi Minh Trail. They were just doing what they were told, trying to kill or capture the American airman, probably scared shitless. I was fairly certain, now, that they didn't know what the fuck they were doing.

But I did, because I was an American Fighting Man. I jumped up from behind the bush and gave my best Johnny Rebel war yell. I pointed my gun at the gomers, pulled the trigger, and held it while I fanned the hammer like I had seen in a movie of Ed McGivern. I fanned through all six rounds in about two seconds, flipped open the chamber and reloaded on the run.

The gomers froze for a split second and then turned tail and ran as fast as they could. I fired off five more rounds, saving that one last round, the one I would use on myself if I needed to.

It was time to get the fuck out of this area.

"Spad, Covey 218 Alpha. The gomers have my position. I'm moving to the north."

"Roger, Alpha. We're bringing in some salad and gravel, and we're going to have to put it right on top of you."

Salad was the code word for tear gas, actually CS gas. I'd been exposed to CS gas once before, when I was a teenager, and it was a real bitch. I had sent away through the mail for a tear-gas pen-gun that I had seen advertised in Field and Stream magazine. When I received it, I inserted the tear gas cartridge, cocked the built-in hammer, and fired it, pointing it away from myself.

I had expected the gas to just hiss out of the pen-gun, like in the spy movies. Instead, it sounded exactly like a gun shot. And I hadn't planned on the effects of the wind. The gas blew back onto me, and I had a terrible, choking feeling. My eyes burned so badly I couldn't open them, and they remained blood red for the rest of the day. Getting gassed was going to be no fun, but at least I'd be prepared. The gomers wouldn't be ready, and while they were choking I would be able to put some distance between them and me. Plus, they wouldn't be able to see me because of the gas.

Gravel was the code word for miniature air-dropped land mines. There were thousands of them in a gravel attack. They were about two inches long, and looked like ravioli made of canvas. They took about five minutes to arm, and then would detonate if anybody stepped on them. They weren't usually lethal, but could blow off a limb and really slow the gomers down. A great choice.

"Roger, I'm ready."

I unzipped my flight suit from the top and tucked my face as deep into it as I could. My nose was about two inches from my armpit. Boy, I really stunk! If I didn't get picked up soon, the gomers would probably be able to find me by smell alone.

A flight of F-4s came over and dropped their ordnance, right on top of me. First, the gravel, then the gas. I took a big breath from my armpit, squinted my eyes and took off running to the north, as fast as I could. I stepped on some of the gravel but, as advertised, the mines hadn't yet armed.

Even with my eyes squeezed as tight as I could get them and still see, they burned like crazy. And my throat and lungs were on fire. After about a hundred meters, I had to stop and pour some water into my eyes from my remaining flask. Then I drank the rest. That was the last of my water, and my throat still burned like crazy.

8

August 3, 1969

I took out my URC-64. I didn't need to whisper any more, since the gomers knew where I was. I just needed to get the fuck out of there. My throat was so dry I could hardly talk.

"This is Covey 218 Alpha. The gomers are really close by and after me. I need a pickup, now!"

Spad came back, "This doesn't sound like Alpha."

Then I heard Vince, my old Academy roommate, on the radio.

"Spad 1, this is Jolly 22. Let me take care of this one."

"Roger, Jolly 22," Spad 1 replied, "go ahead."

Vince came on the radio, "Covey 218 Alpha, authenticate oh dash nine-six, fast, neat, average."

If there was ever a way to tell if someone was

a zoomie, it was through the secret handshake of the Form 0-96. At the Academy, every meal ended with one of the doolies at the table filling out the Food Acceptability Report, officially known as the USAFA Form 0-96. Although the form had several possible responses, there were standard answers that were always used, unless the meal or service was unusually good or bad.

Service of Food: Fast

Waiter Service: Neat

Portion Served: Average

Personnel Attitude: Friendly

Beverage: Good

Meal Considered: Good

I keyed the Transmit switch on the URC-64. "Friendly, good, good."

"Authentication complete!" Vince transmitted, "Jolly 22 is good for the pickup. We have a visual on you, Alpha, but we need you to relocate. I want you to move 200 meters from Mitchell Hall to Arnold Hall."

Even if the gomers were listening, there was no way they would know their way around the Air Force Academy. Mitchell Hall was the dining facility, at the eastern end of the cadet buildings. Arnold Hall was the building where all social functions were held, nestled up against the Rampart Range of the Rocky Mountains, at the west end.

I grabbed my lensatic compass again, took a bearing, and headed west at a full run. I could hear the gravel going off behind me, sounding like firecrackers, followed by the sound of gomers screaming. And I heard more automatic weapons fire. I increased my pace.

I could hear the whop, whop, whop of Jolly 22 hovering over the pickup point, just ahead, out of sight. As I crested the last hill before the pickup area, I ran headfirst into Condom Boy.

G. E. Nolly

9

August 3, 1969

When I was in high school, in 1962, I worked part-time in my uncle's convenience store. Unlike almost every other convenience store, Uncle Harry's store didn't hide the condoms behind the counter. They were on a display rack near the back of the store.

One day, when I was alone at the register, a young Asian boy, maybe 15 years old, came into the store. I couldn't help but notice him. He had very prominent cheekbones and extremely slanted eyes. He wandered around toward the back of the store, picking up a few things and looking at them, then putting them back and walking around with his hands in his pockets. After a while, he walked over to the door to leave.

I could see that something didn't look right. Just as he was about to leave, I walked up to him.

"What's that in your pocket?"

He had a deer-in-the-headlights look.

"I, I don't have anything."

"Empty your pockets," I demanded.

He hung his head and sheepishly emptied his pockets onto the counter. He had a few dollars in one pocket, and a new package of Trojan lubricated condoms in his other pocket.

"So, what's this?"

"Please, mister, I'm sorry. It's just, I was embarrassed to buy prophylactics. I'll pay for them. Please don't tell my parents."

I felt sorry for the kid. I went to the back of the store, grabbed a couple more packs of condoms, and handed them to him.

"Here you go, kid. These are on me. But no more stealing, got it?"

"Yes, sir. Thank you, sir."

After that, I saw the kid every now and then, and he was always was nice and respectful. And he never stole from us again.

I even helped him with his homework a few times. He had an Asian name I couldn't pronounce, so I called him Condom Boy. But I never called him that in front of anyone else. It was our little inside joke. I liked the kid.

I never told Uncle Harry about Condom Boy, and I paid for the condoms myself that day.

The gomer I ran into at the top of the hill was the spitting image of Condom Boy, but older. Maybe it was because, in all honesty, most of these Southeast Asians all looked alike to me. He wasn't wearing an NVA uniform. He was in black pajamas and had a black headband. I was pretty sure he was Pathet Lao.

And he had a really big machete.

When we came upon each other, we were both surprised. There was a pause, perhaps a second or two, then he yelled something, raised his machete, and lunged toward me.

I drew my pistol and fired my last bullet at Condom Boy, the bullet I had been saving for myself. It struck him in his left eye, and his head virtually exploded.

G. E. Nolly

10

August 3, 1969

I was prepared for the sound of the pistol shot. I was prepared for the recoil. I was even prepared to kill another human being. I just wasn't prepared for the smell.

All of the typical sensations from the firing range were there – the loud report, the smell of gunpowder, the slight residual smell of solvent from the last cleaning, the faint haze from the burning gunpowder. But this was different. I was close up and personal when I shot Condom Boy. When his head exploded, there was an overpowering, sickening smell of shit, vomit and raw meat.

And I was totally unprepared for his blood and brains to splash on me. The sensation was overpowering. My head was spinning, but I had to move on or risk joining Condom Boy in the afterworld. I took off at a full-speed run, while attempting to return my empty pistol to my holster. My hand was slippery from the blood and brains, and the gun slipped out and fell to the jungle floor. I kept running. Finally the helicopter was in sight.

The jungle penetrator hoist was almost fully lowered to the ground. I knew from snake school that I had to let it touch the ground, to avoid getting a shock from static electricity build-up. It seemed to take an eternity to travel the final six inches to the ground. It touched.

I pulled the seat down and tugged on the velcro strap to release the safety belt. I sat down on the seat and placed the belt under my arms and fastened it around my chest. I started to give the hoist operator a thumbs-up, but I was already ascending and the Jolly was now swiftly moving out of the area.

Suddenly, the tree line surrounding the pickup area exploded in automatic weapons fire. I could hear the bullets whizzing past me, and could see and hear some of them impacting the side of the chopper. The machine gunner in the chopper was returning withering fire toward the tree line. I hugged the jungle penetrator and held on for dear life.

I was finally all the way up to the chopper door. I remembered from our instruction at snake school that I shouldn't try to help the PJ get me into the chopper, so I just held onto the penetrator. Everything seemed to be happening in slow motion. And in slow motion I saw the elation in the PJ's face turn to horror as a round from an AK-47 ripped into me.

The pain felt exactly like when I was pledging a fraternity in high school in 1959. All of us – the pledges – had to perform menial tasks for the fraternity brothers, and we were constantly being graded on our performance. Then, at the fraternity meetings every Sunday, we would pay for our transgressions. We would be paddled for every infraction, and the fraternity brothers would take turns hitting us in the ass with large wooden paddles, trying to make us cry.

One of the senior fraternity brothers, Doug Mattson, was well-known for his ability to make even the most stoic pledge burst into tears. It was my turn to be paddled by Doug, and I assumed the position. I bent over, grabbed my balls to protect them, and waited for the sting of the paddle. I was prepared to immediately jump to a standing position and recite the mandatory, "Thank you, sir, may I have another?"

But something happened. Instead of hitting me square in the ass with the flat surface of the paddle, Doug hit just the left side of my ass . And he hit it with the edge of the paddle. I was instantly flooded with pain, but I didn't cry. I passed out.

That was the pain I felt when I got shot in the ass as I was being hoisted into the chopper on the jungle penetrator. This time, I didn't pass out. I vomited. All over my flight suit, all over the jungle penetrator. Some got in the chopper, too.

The vomit didn't faze the PJ or the onboard medic. They were all business as they pulled me in. The PJ handed me a canteen, and I wanted to drink the entire contents. I gulped it frantically. He pried it out of my hands after I finished about half.

I found myself sobbing uncontrollably as soon as I was in the chopper. The long-term adrenaline dump had really taken a toll on my body. As the PJ cleaned me up, the medic tended to my wound. He cut off the bottom of my flight suit, gave me an injection in my other ass cheek, and the pain started to fade. The last thing I remember was saying, "My *daruma*," and then I slowly blacked out. As I slipped out of consciousness, I could still hear enemy rounds hitting our chopper, and I could hear the return fire from the door gunner. And then all of the sounds faded to silence.

11

August 3, 1969

I cycled into and out of consciousness several times as I was taken to NKP Air Base, Thailand, processed at the NKP Hospital, and then transferred to a C-9 Nightingale med-evac aircraft. The memories are a blur.

I awoke briefly aboard the C-9. I was securely belted onto a stretcher fastened to the side of the cabin. I glanced around in the dim light and saw other stretchers. There was an unconscious burn victim in one, and a female, probably in her 20s, with bandages on her head, in another.

When the Flight Nurse saw me looking around, she came up to me. She was a Lieutenant Colonel, probably in her early forties, just a little younger than my mom.

She gently brushed my hair and said, "Are you feeling okay, sweetie?"

I felt like I was being caressed by my mom.

And right then I really needed nurturing. I started to cry, and turned my head so she wouldn't see. She gently brushed my hair again as she stuck a hypodermic needle into my IV, and then everything faded.

When I next awoke I was in the Officer's Ward at the Cam Ranh Air Base Hospital.

12

August 4, 1969

I woke up in extreme pain, localized to my left buttock. My whole body was sore, like I had just had an intense workout. It was the kind of whole-body soreness I had felt the second day of basic training.

As I opened my eyes, I saw a doctor and nurse standing by my bed. I had tubes attached to me in a couple of places: an IV in my left arm, and a urinary catheter.

The doctor spoke first.

"How are you feeling, Lieutenant Hancock?"

"I feel like I just got beat up. And I feel like I got shot in the ass."

The doctor looked at the nurse.

"Sense of humor intact. That's a good sign." Then he turned to me. "I'm Doctor Wilbanks. I'm going to have Nurse Schmidt remove your IV and catheter, and I want you to try to get up and walk around as much as you can. The surgery to remove the bullet went extremely well, and you should heal quickly. But you'll need to stay here in the hospital until you've finished your antibiotic treatment, ten days."

"Where am I?"

"Oh, I thought you knew. You're at the 12th USAF Combat Staging Hospital at Cam Ranh Air Base. This is probably the best location in all of Vietnam, and you're free to go anywhere you want on base. In fact, I *want* you go walk around the base. You need to keep moving to stretch out your gluteus maximus muscles."

"If you go to the beach, though," he added, "I want you to stay out of the water. I don't want you to get your injury infected. Any questions?"

"One, actually. How soon will I get back on flying status?"

"That will be up to the Flight Surgeon at DaNang. Unless you're requesting to go back to the States now." He glanced at my chart. "You're in the Air Force, so if you want to return to the States, we can make that happen."

"Hell no. I haven't finished my tour, and I have an extension request in the system so I can participate in a special mission."

"Okay. I'm just required to tell you your options. Nurse Schmidt will take care of you now. If you need anything at all, she's here for you. I'll see you tomorrow."

With that, Dr. Wilbanks walked away. Clearly, he was all business. Nurse Schmidt, on the other hand, was a lot warmer. She pulled portable cloth privacy partitions up around my bed, and pulled down the sheet that was covering me.

I was naked in the bed, and looked down and saw the catheter. I had never been catheterized before. When I looked down, I was shocked. My penis had never looked so small, shriveled to about half its normal size. She gently removed my catheter.

"It's not usually swollen that big," I quipped.

"Sense of humor," she smiled, as she removed the IV. "That's a good sign." She looked me in the eyes. "You've been in shock, from being shot and from the surgery. When you're in shock, the body reduces blood flow to the extremities. It will return to normal size soon."

"It wouldn't hurt," she added with a smile, "to try a little manipulation."

She motioned to the small cabinet next to my bed, with a new set of underwear and light blue pajamas stacked on top.

"Here's your new uniform. As long as you're wearing the pajamas, you get priority everywhere on base, including the MARS station. Be sure not to remove this wristband," she touched the plastic identification band on my left wrist, "and don't get your scar wet. I'll help you when you need to shower."

I nodded. "What do I call you, Nurse Schmidt, Major, what?"

"Whichever you want." She glanced off to my left, at the beds along my wall in the open bay. "The Marines always call me Major. They're big into using rank instead of name. I'm Air Force, like you."

"One last thing," she commented. "As soon as you start to feel pain, I want you to take these pain pills." She held up a small plastic bottle of pills, removed one, then put the bottle back on my cabinet. She handed me the pill and a glass of water. I swallowed the pill, and the pain started subsiding almost immediately.

"They're Tylox, Tylenol plus codeine. No heroics. If you wait until the pain is bad, you'll need a lot more pain meds."

"Okay. Understood."

"Remember, no heroics."

"Yes, Ma'am."

I slowly got out of bed and put on the new jockey shorts and the light blue pajamas. There were two sets of footwear under my bed – a set of rubber flip-flops like the gomers wore, and a new pair of Converse sneakers with a pair of athletic socks. I picked up the sneakers and looked inside. They had selected the right size.

I opened the drawer of the cabinet and looked inside. I was ecstatic – all of the contents from the pockets of my flight suit were in the drawer. My Rolex, my wallet, still sticky from my blood, my dog tags, my binoculars and, most importantly, my *daruma*.

I put on my dog tags, slipped on the flip-flops, and walked around the ward. There were about fifteen beds, arranged along the walls, with the heads against the walls. Three of the beds were obviously unoccupied, with no sheets. Every bed that had sheets on it had a clipboard with medical information in a small wire basket attached to the foot. There were only five patients in their beds. The others were probably in the television room or out around the base.

I saw a young guy, probably around 22, reading a magazine in the first occupied bed I came to. As I approached, he put aside his magazine.

"Hi," I said, holding out my hand, "I'm Hamilton Hancock." There was no need for everyone here to call me Hamfist. "You can call me Ham."

"Hi, Lieutenant," he said, shaking my hand, "I'm Lieutenant Royce."

"Marine, right?"

"Affirmative. How'd you know?"

"Just a lucky guess," I answered. "What're you in for?" As soon as I asked, I realized I sounded like the dialog from a cheesy prison movie.

"Six months ago I took an AK round through both legs. I'm based at Camp DaNang, and was out on patrol in Hoi An. One shot, broke both femurs." He swung his legs over the side of the bed and gingerly stood up. "I just got rid of the crutches last week."

"You've been here six months, and they didn't send you back to the States?"

"Marine policy. If you're going to have three months retainability in-country after you're fit for duty, you stay here. I got hit right after completing my first month. I'll be going back into the field in about two weeks."

I was amazed at the difference between the way the various services handled combat casualties. In the Air Force, if we got hurt, at all, we had the option to go back to the States. The Army and Marines were much more strict.

I walked around the ward and made my introductions to the other guys who were there. I saw one bed with privacy curtains all around it at the end of the room. Just after I noticed it, a middle-aged Vietnamese woman came into our ward, walked up to the curtained partition, and went inside.

"What's going on over there?" I asked Royce.

"Oh," he answered, looking toward the curtained bed, "that's General Ng. He's one of the highest-ranking generals in the Vietnamese Air Force. He was flying an A-1 and took a serious hit. When they wheeled him in here three weeks ago, they didn't think he would make it. He seems to get special treatment. His wife spends all day with him."

Suddenly, I really needed to find a toilet. Number two.

"Which way to the head?"

"Through that door, on the left."

"Thanks."

I went out of the ward, found the latrine, and entered one of the stalls. It took a bit of maneuvering to sit on the toilet without my surgery scar hurting, but I finally found a position that wasn't too painful.

There was a magazine rack on the inside of the stall door, and a selection of magazines. Playboy, Gent, Penthouse. I picked out a magazine and started reading.

Maybe even manipulating. Nurse's orders.

13

August 4, 1969

As I was leaving the latrine, I saw my reflection in the mirror. I looked terrible. I needed a shave, my face was gaunt, my eyes sunken. I looked like I had lost twenty pounds, maybe more. I unbuttoned my pajama top and looked at my stomach.

I could actually see my abs, for the first time in years. The last time I had abs, I was a gymnast at the Academy. That was a lifetime ago.

There were some disposable razors in the latrine, and I grabbed one and shaved. I looked a little better. A little.

When I returned to the ward, I went back over to Royce's bedside.

"Lieutenant, I discovered a great weight-loss system. When I get back to the world, I'm going to market it and make a million dollars."

"Really? What's your system?"

"I'm going to parachute the fat people into Laos and let gomers chase them for two days."

"Very funny. You know, they say that getting your sense of humor back is a really good sign."

"So I've been told."

There was something that was gnawing at me, and I decided to discuss it with Lieutenant Royce.

"Lieutenant, you said you were in-country for a while before you got injured."

"That's right."

"Did you make contact with the enemy a lot?"

"Quite a bit, usually short encounters. Like when I got shot. One minute we're patrolling in a rice paddy, the next minute all hell breaks loose, then it's over. Why do you ask?"

"Well, I've been in-country for seven months, and I've had a lot of contact, probably killed a lot of gomers, but always from a mile away or more. Because of the way we do our job, we never really know how many people we've killed, but when you see a truck park explode with secondaries, you can figure you took out quite a few bad guys. But we don't get body counts like you guys on the ground."

"Body count is just the way we keep score,"

Royce commented.

"Okay. Here's what's bothering me. I killed a gomer a few days ago, up close. Really close. I blew his fucking head off. He's probably the hundredth gomer I've killed, but this one really bothers me."

"That's because you were so close when you killed him," Royce replied. "When I first got to DaNang, I took a patrol out, and we made contact with the enemy, they were maybe 500 meters away. I used the BAR, squeezed off one round, and saw a bright red mist where the gomer's head used to be. It was totally impersonal."

"Then, a few days later, we made contact again, this time really close. Face to face. I even had to use my knife. When you kill from close up, it's totally different, especially when you look through their personal effects afterward. You find pictures, letters, all kinds of stuff. And you realize they were just ordinary people. And you ended their lives forever. You took away their futures. But you get used to it. You're not killing them for fun, you're killing them because they're trying to kill you. And, after a while, you even kind of enjoy it, because you're killing off someone who may have ended up killing one of your buddies. You're protecting your comrades. When I was at Annapolis, we studied the art of war."

"You went to Annapolis? What year?"

"I graduated in 1968. Anyway, I learned that Clausewitz said that the ultimate purpose of war is to destroy the enemy's will to fight. That's the macro view, for politicians. For us, the purpose of war is to kill every enemy gomer before he kills you. Like Patton said, 'The object of war is not to die for your country, but to make the other guy die for his'."

"Thanks, Lieutenant," I responded. "You've really helped me get my head on straight. I hadn't thought of it that way before. Protecting my comrades."

He was right. Every gomer I kill is one less gomer to shoot at my squadron-mates. I didn't start this fight, but I was damn well not going to run from it.

I thought back of the Thomas Hardy poem, written about an enemy he had killed in war, World War I. I had been required to memorize it in high school:

Had he and I but met
By some old ancient inn,
We should have set us down to wet
Right many a nipperkin!

Maybe it was because the gomer I killed reminded me so much of Condom Boy, I could picture myself sitting down with him at a bar and having a nipperkin, which my English teacher Mrs. Benson had explained was slightly less than a half pint. Yeah, in a different situation, I could have had a nipperkin with Condom Boy.

14

August 4, 1969

"Let me ask you something," Royce said, "When you went through weapons qualification training, what kind of target did you shoot at?"

"The standard round bulls-eye. Why?"

"Well, when I went through training, we shot at silhouettes of people, rather than bulls-eyes. It helped us get mentally ready to shoot at the enemy. In fact, the Range Officer didn't say, 'Ready on the right, ready on the left ready on the firing line. Commence firing', like they did at the range at Annapolis. He said, 'Ready, kill the fucking gooks. Now fire!' It got us thinking about dehumanizing the enemy and getting mentally ready to fight. Shooting at bulls-eyes doesn't do that."

"Makes sense to me. Thanks. Say, I'm going to go exploring around the base. Doctor's orders. Are you up for a little walk?"

"Not quite yet. Maybe in a day or two. Be

sure to make note of our building number, 3297, so you can find your way back here."

"Okay. See you later."

I put on the athletic socks and changed into the sneakers. Then it occurred to me I had no idea what time of day it was. It might have been morning, might have been early evening.

"Lieutenant Royce, do you know what time it is?"

"It's eleven forty-one, Lieutenant. They'll be serving lunch in the chow hall starting at noon. Or you can go to the O'Club and show them your bracelet, and you can eat there for free."

"Thanks."

I set the time on my Rolex, put it on, and left the ward. I walked outside and checked the number written on the side of the building, so I would be able to find my way back. Building 3297, just like Lieutenant Royce had said. Our building, like every other building, had sandbags stacked up about four feet high around all sides.

One of the first things I noticed when I left the building was that the ground was very sandy. It was almost like I was walking on the beach. I didn't have to walk on the sand, though, because there were sidewalks, some made of concrete and some made of wood, like boardwalks.

This was the perfect place for recuperation. There was a warm sea breeze, the base was right on the ocean, and there was a tranquil, idyllic mood that pervaded everything. The area was beautiful, there was a gorgeous view of the ocean, and the whole place had the feel of Hawaii. In fact, it reminded me a lot of Fort DeRussey, the military facility I had visited in Honolulu during one of my all-too-short summer vacations from the Academy. It seemed so peaceful. So different from DaNang.

I walked around for a while, learning the geography of the base, and eventually ended up at the Officers Club. I considered going into the bar and getting a beer, but I wasn't sure if I could drink alcohol with my medication, so I just had an iced tea with my sandwich. The waiter copied the information from my wrist band, and I didn't need to pay, just like Lieutenant Royce had said. Before I left, I asked for directions to the MARS facility.

The Military Affiliate Radio Station allowed GIs to make long-distance calls using the services of ham radio operators all over the world. And, just like I'd been told, the Sergeant running the operation motioned me to the head of the line when he saw I was in hospital pajamas.

I was really anxious to get a call to my mother, to let her know I was okay. I was concerned that maybe the Air Force had reported me missing, and she would be beside herself.

There were about a dozen guys waiting to make calls, and the calls were piped over the loudspeaker, so everyone could hear everything that was said. Any degree of intimacy was impossible.

The ham radio operator that we made contact with was in Fort Walton Beach, so it wasn't even a long distance call to my mom's house in Pensacola. A man answered. I immediately recognized Phil's voice.

"Hi Phil. This is Ham. Is Mom there? Over."

"Dorothy. It's Ham! Yes, on the phone." In the background I heard my mom wailing. Phil said, "She'll be right here." He didn't say "Over," so Mom's phone was still in the Transmit mode.

"Ham! Is that you? Are you okay? Over." She was crying so uncontrollably, I had a hard time understanding her.

"Yes, Mom. I'm fine. Over."

"The Colonel who came here said you were missing in action. Over." She had calmed down somewhat, but was still sobbing a lot.

"It was just a mix-up. I didn't land at the base where they expected me, so they reported me missing. No big deal. Over."

"You never were good at lying to me," she was no longer crying, "like when you were in high school and told me you had gotten rid of all those nasty magazines. Then I looked in your closet. Over."

The crowd in the MARS waiting room exploded in laughter.

"Okay, Mom. I got shot down. Just like Phil and just like Dad. And just like both of them, I got rescued. It was really no big deal. I'm just sorry they notified you and made you worry. Over."

"You know I worry about you all the time, no matter what. But I feel a lot better hearing your voice. Stay safe, Honey. I love you. Over."

"I love you too, Mom. Goodbye. Over."

I really wanted to call Sam, but there were a lot of guys waiting to call home, so I decided I'd come back later. I headed back to my ward. My scar was starting to hurt, a lot. I felt like an idiot for not carrying my Tylox with me.

By the time I got back to the ward, I could hardly walk, and I was sweating profusely. As soon as I walked in, Nurse Schmidt was on me like bees on honey.

"You're in pain, right?"

"Yes, ma'am."

"Did you take a Tylox?"

"No. I forgot to take them with me."

"On the bed, now!"

I climbed into the bed, laying down on my right side. Nurse Schmidt had left the room momentarily, and returned with a large hypodermic needle. She pulled down my pajama bottoms, rubbed an alcohol swab on my ass, about six inches from my scar, and jabbed me with the needle.

"This is morphine. It's what we have to give you to control the pain if you don't catch it in time with the Tylox."

It felt good. I was starting to feel like I was floating. I could get used to this.

"If we give you too much morphine, you'll get addicted. Don't ever leave the ward without your Tylox again." She put my Tylox bottle in the chest pocket of my pajamas. "Carry it with you at all times."

"Yes, ma'am."

I shut my eyes and was immediately asleep.

I woke up a few hours later. Just as I awoke, I saw the orderlies wheeling a gurney in through the door. The patient on the gurney had been severely injured. He had tubes going into and coming out of all parts of his body, and he had huge scars from numerous lacerations, with gigantic stitches holding them closed. It reminded me of Frankenstein's monster.

I looked closer, and realized I recognized the patient. It was Willy Wilson, a pilot who had gone through Hurlburt and FAC-U with me. He was based in Pleiku. I made eye contact with him, and I saw a glint of recognition. All of a sudden, my wound seemed trivial.

G. E. Nolly

15

August 7, 1969

I went over to Willy's bed to see how he was doing. I had tried to visit for the past two days, but there were privacy curtains around him, like General Ng. But today, the curtains were gone.

Most of the tubes were gone, too, and he looked alert.

"Hamilton! What the fuck are you doing here?"

"I got shot down about a week ago, and took an AK round."

"You look okay. Where were you hit?"

I knew this would come up. I had to attack it head-on.

"I got shot in the ass." I pulled down my pajama bottoms and showed him my bandage.

Willy started laughing so hard I thought he might bust his stitches.

"So," I asked, "what happened to you?"

"I was in my hooch, just fell asleep. Two, maybe three nights ago. I'm not really sure what day it is now. Anyway, we had a rocket attack, and one of the rockets made a direct hit on my fucking hooch. Huge flash. Huge explosion."

"At first I didn't feel any pain," he continued, "but I couldn't move. I just laid there, under a bunch of rubble, and I heard the blood gurgling out of my body. And then Moose Myers – you know him? – ran over to what remained of my hooch, picked me up in his arms, and carried me all the way to the hospital. During a fucking rocket attack! Fucking amazing!"

"My God! You're really lucky."

"No, I think the guys who didn't get hit were lucky."

"You have a point."

"Hamilton, let me ask you something. Do you believe in fatalism, you know, when your number is up your number is up?"

"Actually, I do. Why? You too?"

"Well, I didn't think much about it before I got hit by that rocket. But now, when I think about it, there were signs that I was going to be injured."

"What kind of signs?"

"Well, a few weeks ago, the golden BB just missed me, and I think it was s sign I was fated to get hit."

"What happened?"

"I was flying along, solo, on a day mission, when the whole cockpit just exploded in shattered glass and plastic. My right window was gone, my visor was gone, and I couldn't hear anything in my headset. I took off my ballistic helmet and looked inside. There was a groove along the inside of the liner, and my headset wires were broken."

"I put the helmet back on," he continued, "and flew back to Pleiku. I had to do a radio-out pattern. Flew down initial, rocking my wings, looking for the green light from the tower, the whole bit. After I landed I took my helmet to the Life Support shop, and we figured out what had happened. An AK round came in through the right window, shattered my visor, went *inside* my helmet, and went all the way around in my ballistic helmet. It just barely missed taking off my nose. Ever since then, I felt like it was just a matter of time until I actually got hurt. I think I was fated to get injured."

"Well, to be honest," I said, "I've always had

a feeling that there's something going on that's well beyond our control. We had a guy at DaNang who flew like he didn't give a shit about what happened to him. He'd been passed over for Major, and figured he needed to get some combat decorations to be more competitive. He did crazy things, got into pissing contests with 23s, and he never got a scratch."

"We had another guy," I continued, "who was *desperate* to finish his tour alive. All he could talk about was getting home to his wife and son. He had a Date of Separation and was going to get out of the Air Force and work for his father-in-law's furniture store."

"He told me he was thinking of calling in sick for his Champagne Flight, and not pressing his luck on one last mission. He had this sickening feeling he wouldn't make it back alive. I told him it was his choice. Nobody would think anything bad about him if he canceled. Damn if I was going to pressure anyone to go fly if they didn't feel up to it. But he was afraid we'd think he was a pussy."

"Well," I continued, "there was a thunderstorm at DaNang the night before his Champagne Flight, and Maintenance installed control locks in the flight controls of all the airplanes.

Willy interrupted, "You're not going to tell me he took off with the controls locked!"

"Yeah," I answered, "he apparently didn't do a control check before takeoff, or he would have discovered it. He made an intersection takeoff, and got about 300 feet in the air before the airplane stalled out and spun in. The really shitty thing is, if he had used the whole runway, he would have had enough runway ahead of him to abort the takeoff when he found the controls wouldn't move. He was killed during the crash."

Willy and I just looked at each other, not knowing what else to say.

"New subject," he said, "You're a zoomie, aren't you?"

"Yeah. Why?"

"Well, there was a classmate of yours at Pleiku who really dishonored the Academy."

"Who? What happened?"

"A guy we called Popeye. Last name Koffman."

I knew exactly who he was talking about. Bill Koffman had been in a few of my classes at the Academy. He had two eyes that were totally different sizes, and I often wondered how he passed the Academy physical, let alone the eye exam for entrance to pilot training. It looked funny as hell, but apparently it didn't affect his vision one bit.

Bill seemed like a nice enough guy. Some of the guys had called him Popeye behind his back, but I couldn't believe anyone called him that to his face. Then again, in the pilot community, especially in the combat environment, we could be a bit insensitive.

"Popeye had arrived at Pleiku a few weeks ahead of me," he continued, "and he was really a gung-ho warrior. He was very animated with his hands as he would tell me about seeing the concussion shock waves whenever he put in an airstrike. He even showed me the snub-nose revolver he carried in the leg pocket of his flight suit, in addition to the issued Smith & Wesson. A real warrior."

"Then, he flew his first night mission. You know how we see all the ground fire at night. Well, he really got hosed. Fourth of July hosed. It shook him up. The next day, he put in his papers as a conscious objector."

"Bill became a CO?" I asked incredulously.

"Yeah, CO, as in the first two letters of the word 'coward'. They assigned him to the 'hearts and minds' program, you know, going out to villages and giving candy bars to kids, that kind of stuff. And they kept him at Pleiku for a total of 181 days. That gave him credit for a complete tour in Vietnam, and then he got an Honorable Discharge. Honorable Discharge. What bullshit!"

I was really disappointed to hear that about a classmate. Apparently, Bill hadn't really learned the intrinsic lesson of the American Fighting Man's Code of Conduct.

During one of my walks around the base the previous day, I heard some little kids laughing. It was coming from the ward next to ours, building 3299. I stuck my head in to look around. I saw a nurse, a Major.

"Is it okay to visit?" I asked.

"Absolutely. The kids love to meet new people. These are the real victims of this war. Most of these kids were injured by rocket attacks. Be gentle with them."

There were about twenty kids there, most of them infants. There were seven who were between four and seven years old. All of them were badly injured. One kid was missing his left hand. Another only had one eye. Several were on crutches. I wanted to wrap my arms around each one, to make the pain go away. It just wasn't fair what was happening to these innocent kids.

And still, they smiled. There was no self-pity. Most of the kids acted like there was nothing wrong. I spent about an hour with the kids. I couldn't understand a word they said, and they couldn't understand me.

But I was able to teach them the names of the seven dwarfs. Happy, Dopey, Sleepy, Grumpy, Sneezy, Bashful, Doc. We had a contest to see which kid could recite the names the fastest. It was great to see them laugh. It was a good feeling to leave them smiling.

I went to the BX and bought about a dozen Hershey bars. The clerk at the BX copied the information from my wrist band, and I left and headed back to building 3299. I had been gone for about an hour.

The kids were happy to see me again. The nurse said, "The kids have something to show you."

One by one, each kid recited one of the seven dwarf names.

"Happy."

"Dopey."

"Sleepy."

"Grumpy."

"Sneezy."

"Bashful."

"Doc."

"They want you to call them by the names they learned," the nurse said.

"With pleasure," I said. I turned to the kids, "I'm so proud of all of you!"

I reached into my bag, withdrew the Hershey bars, and started handing them out. Suddenly, the nurse ran up to me and grabbed the candy from me.

"What the hell are you doing?" she demanded.

"I'm giving the kids candy." It was what GIs did in every war movie I'd ever seen as a kid.

"Lieutenant, I appreciate the intent, but these kids are all taking medications, and the caffeine in chocolate can have an adverse interaction. Please don't do this again."

"I'm really sorry, Major."

I stayed around for a little while and practiced associating each of the seven dwarf names with the seven kids. Then I left. I knew I should have checked with the nurse before giving the kids anything. I felt like an idiot. I needed to talk to someone who would not be judgmental. I needed to talk to Sam.

I had been trying to place a MARS call to

Sam for the past two days, and didn't get through because they couldn't find any ham radio operators in Japan on the air at the time. After dinner I went back to the MARS station for another try.

It was just getting dark when I arrived at the station. As usual, I went to the head of the line, and this time, we made contact with a ham radio operator in Japan, right in Tokyo. I placed the call, and anxiously waited to hear her voice. A female answered, and my heart started beating faster as soon as I heard Sam's voice.

"Sam, it's so good to hear your voice. We're talking on a radio call, so you need to say the word O-V-E-R when you finish each sentence. Over."

"Ham! I was so worried about you. When I called your squadron, they said you hadn't returned from your flight. Over."

I needed to have a conversation about OPSEC – Operations Security – and COMSEC – Communication Security – with the squadron Admin Clerk. He should've just said I wasn't there.

"I had a little problem in the target area, but I'm okay now. I'm not at DaNang right now, I'm at a beautiful base further south. Cam Ranh

Bay. But you can still write to me at my old address, because I'll be heading back to DaNang in about a week. Over."

"Were you hurt? Over."

"Very minor scrape. Nothing to worry about. But I have to tell you, the experience really got me thinking about what's important to me. And what's important to me right now is to tell you I love you. Over."

"I love you too, Ham. I can't stop thinking about you. Over."

Cheers from the peanut gallery.

"I'll call you again real soon, honey. I love you. Good bye. Over."

"I love you, too. Good bye. Over."

There. I said it. When I was down in the jungle, thinking I may die at any time, my only regret was not telling Sam how I felt about her. As I returned to the ward, I was walking on cloud nine.

Just as I approached the door of the ward, I saw a dark figure running from building 3299, toward our ward. Then the door of building 3299 exploded.

16

August 7, 1969

Just as building 3299 was engulfed in flames, the attack siren sounded. I heard other explosions in the distance, and it was immediately clear to me that the base was under sapper attack. And the dark figure running toward me, and my ward, was one of the sappers.

In our Unarmed Combat classes at the Academy, the instructors emphasized that it was important to use the element of surprise, to keep the enemy off balance. I gave a loud yell, what in karate we called a *kiyai*, and clapped my hands together, once, as loud as I could. It seemed to startle the sapper.

While he was stopped, I quickly knelt down, grabbed a handful of sand, and threw it in his face. He was temporarily blinded, and I wasn't going to waste the opportunity.

I kicked him in the balls as hard as I could,

and he doubled over. Then I delivered a knife-edge hand strike to his neck, right at the front of his windpipe. It worked just as advertised. He started choking.

I remembered our instructor saying, "The windpipe is like soft copper tubing. You can crush it with a well-placed blow and there's nothing anyone can do to prevent your adversary from asphyxiating. Never, and I mean never, use it in a fight unless your life is on the line."

I was pretty sure this qualified as justified use of the windpipe attack. The sapper was holding his throat, clearly unable to breathe. I went behind him, grabbed his head with both hands, and gave a forceful twist. I wanted to twist his fucking head completely off. I felt a snap and the sapper fell limp to the ground.

Royce had been correct. It was easier to kill a second time. And, when I saw what this bastard had done, it felt good.

I ran into 3299. There was blood and debris everywhere, and kids were screaming. The lights at the front of the ward were out. The only illumination was from the battery-powered emergency lights that remained on the far wall. Two nurses and a doctor were performing triage, treating the kids who were going to live, ignoring anyone with more serious, possibly mortal, wounds. There was a lot of shouting of medical terms I didn't understand. I felt totally helpless. I didn't know a thing about combat first aid. I just knew I needed to stay out of everyone's way.

I saw Grumpy lying near the door in a huge pool of blood. He was still breathing, just barely. Short, shallow breaths. I sat on the floor and cradled him, softly weeping as I rocked him forward on his journey to Heaven.

G. E. Nolly

17

August 9, 1969

The past two days had been tough. We mourned our losses, buried our dead, and tried to rebuild. Everyone participated. Patients were relocated to wards that hadn't been damaged. Those of us who were able took turns standing guard.

The sappers had attacked 19 of the 84 buildings on base, and had totally destroyed four. Ninety-eight people on base were wounded, and three were killed, including Grumpy. The unanticipated casualty, however, was our innocence.

Cam Ranh, prior to the attack, had been placid. We had a gorgeous facility, incredible view, and friendly local environment. That was now gone. None of us would ever look at Cam Ranh Bay the same again.

But, like when Mitch had been shot down early in my tour, the world didn't stop turning.

Life went on. There were times when we smiled, even occasionally laughed. At first, when we found humor, we felt guilty. Then, we simply embraced the moment.

On this day, General Ng's wife was wildly giggling behind the curtains. Nurse Schmidt peeked in to see if everything was okay, and she emerged smiling.

Royce knew Nurse Schmidt better than any of the other patients, and he appointed himself the ambassador to find out what was going on. He went over to Nurse Schmidt and they whispered for a few seconds. Then Royce went up to each patient and briefly chatted.

Finally, he made his way to me.

"Okay, Lieutenant," I said, "what's going on?"

"General Ng is doing much better." He paused for effect. "He just had his first hard-on since getting injured."

When Mrs. Ng appeared from behind the curtain, we all applauded. She smiled, looked down at the ground, and quickly left the room.

After lunch, Nurse Schmidt advised me that there was going to be an award ceremony later in the afternoon. Along with twelve other patients, I was going to receive my Purple

Heart Medal.

"There is a news team from Tokyo here to film the aftermath of the attack, and they will be filming the awards ceremony also. They requested an interview with you afterward. They asked for you by name."

"Should I talk to them?" I asked.

"The Base Commander said it would be advisable." She paused. "That's short-hand for: you really need to do it."

"Understood."

Part of me was looking forward to meeting some people form Tokyo, and practicing the Japanese I'd learned from Sam. Part of me was really apprehensive about being on television. Well, it couldn't be any worse than getting chased around Laos by the NVA or fighting in hand-to-hand combat with a sapper.

The award ceremony was very straight-forward. All of us were in our light blue pajamas, and we stood at attention as the Colonel pinned our Purple Hearts on our chests. There was a Japanese news team filming the entire event.

After the ceremony, the news team moved their cameras closer, while some assistants applied makeup to a middle-aged Japanese man who was obviously the news anchor. He was barking commands in Japanese to his helpers, and they were very deferential to him. They seemed afraid of him. Instantly, I didn't like him.

He looked in my direction and said, "Transrator come soon."

I nodded.

Then the translator arrived, a good-looking woman. No, a beautiful woman. Her hair was pulled back in a pony-tail, and she was wearing no makeup. She was gorgeous.

I did a double-take. It couldn't be, but it was – it was Sam! She locked eyes with me and blinked a few times. Then she bowed slightly and handed me a business card.

"Herro. My name Sachiko Yamada. I transrate for Mister Onishi. This is my *meishi*." She looked into my eyes and blinked again.

I was totally confused. I looked at the *meishi*, and it said "Sachiko Yamada". I knew there was some form of charade going on here, and I could see it was important to Sam for me to play along.

During the next ten minutes, Mr. Onishi asked questions in Japanese, and then Sam asked them to me in heavily accented English.

They were general, soft-ball questions, asking me about what airplane I fly, what a FAC does, how long have I been in Vietnam, was I injured badly. Very bland questions.

Then, totally unexpected, Mr. Onishi got a stern look on his face and asked his next question. Sam translated.

"Why do you participate in a war against Asians who simply want to reunite into one peaceful country?"

I was shocked.

"This is not a war against Asians. We are protecting the people of South Vietnam from the violent aggression of the Communists in North Vietnam."

Sam started translating, and I didn't wait for her to pause. I knew she could translate on the fly, and I continued talking.

"You want to talk about war against Asians? Take a look at building 3299, where a Vietnamese child was killed two days ago by the North Vietnamese. The rest of the children in that ward were all injured by indiscriminate attacks on civilians. You want to talk about a war against Asians? Take a look at Cam Ranh Bay beach. You'll see gun emplacements, pill boxes, that are left over from when the

Imperial Japanese Army occupied this entire country and all of Asia."

He replied, "Today is the anniversary of the brutal American attack on Nagasaki. I can see that you don't care about that. I can see that you hate the Japanese."

I was really pissed now. I looked right at the camera.

"You're obviously uninformed. I don't hate the Japanese. I was in Japan just one week ago. I love the Japanese. The woman I love was born in Japan, and is a samurai descendant. She showed me a *tsuba* that she inherited that once belonged to the samurai Musashi. I plan to return to Japan in December. Mr. Onishi, you don't know what the hell you're talking about."

"But," I continued, "I can tell you don't like Americans. Let me tell you something. Unlike the Japanese Imperial Army, which subjugated the people they conquered, the Americans didn't enslave Japan. We rebuilt your country. With our tax dollars. And I'll tell you something else, Mr. Onishi. If the Americans hadn't dragged Japan kicking and screaming into the twentieth century, there would be no way a person like you, who obviously is not of samurai descent, would be able to get a job as a newscaster."

He seemed totally flustered. He looked down at his list for one more question.

"How did you get nickname Hamu-fist?"

"My name is Hamilton Hancock. Our nicknames are chosen to sound similar to our names. I could be called either Hamfist or Handjob."

Mr. Onishi bypassed the translator and asked me directly, "What is mean hando-job?"

I smiled to Sam, looked directly at the camera and, with my right hand, made a motion like I was masturbating.

Onishi barked a command to his assistants, turned on his heel, and walked away. The red light on the camera blinked off. Sam was working hard to stifle a giggle.

Before she left, Sam said, "Prease to keep my *meishi*." She gave a slight bow, and followed Onishi.

After they all left, I once again looked at the *meishi*. I turned it over, and saw "9 p.m. DV Quarters, apartment 105."

I looked at my Rolex. It was 7 p.m. The two hours until nine o'clock seemed to take forever.

I knew where the Distinguished Visitor Quarters were located, and had no trouble getting there. I knocked softly on the door to apartment 105. Sam answered the door, wearing a white terry robe.

"Sam, I don't really under..." Before I could finish my question, she grabbed the lapels of my pajamas, pulled me into the room, shut the door and planted a hard, passionate kiss on me. Before I knew it, her robe was on the floor, and she was ripping my pajamas off me.

We made love like a starving man attacking a buffet. We were making up for lost time in the past, and what might be lost time in the future. There was no past, no future. There was only the here and now.

When we were finished, we just lay in bed and looked at each other. Then Sam said, "I'll show you mine if you show me yours."

"What?"

"Your scar."

"Sure." I rolled over and showed her the angry red scar on my ass. The bandage had been off for several days.

"Does it hurt?"

"A little. Mostly, it itches. Now let me see yours."

Sam rolled over onto her stomach, and I saw a scar, about two inches long, in the small of her back.

"It's from the accident I had when I was a kid. I told you about it."

I softly kissed her scar, then I rolled her over and kissed her on her stomach. She had a gorgeous body, and a beautiful stomach. Her navel was adorable. Definitely an "innie".

"I love you so much, Sam," I said, as I kissed her on her navel.

"Lower," she breathed.

I lowered my voice about two octaves to a deep baritone and said, "I love you so much, Sam."

We both laughed uncontrollably and hugged each other.

"That's one of the reasons I love you, Ham. Your sense of humor."

"They tell me it helps."

G. E. Nolly

18

August 10, 1969

It was already past midnight, and I knew I would need to leave soon. We had just spent the past two hours talking about what had transpired in the week since I left Tokyo. It seemed so long ago.

I hadn't planned on talking about it. But Sam had said, "Ham, you look so tired and thin. And you look troubled."

And the flood gates opened. I told her about how terrified I was of getting captured. About saving that last round for myself. About Condom Boy. About the seven dwarfs. About the sapper. About Grumpy.

She listened. She understood.

Then it was time to move on to other subjects.

"I loved the way you put that idiot Onishi in his place."

"What was the deal with the phony name

and the accent?" I asked.

"Actually, it's not a phony name. It's my Japanese name. Like I told you, I was born on base, at Itazuke Air Base in Fukuoka. I got an American birth certificate and citizenship because Daddy is American, but I also got Japanese citizenship and a *koseki shohon* because Mommy is, was, Japanese.

"A what?"

"A *koseki shohon*. It's the equivalent of a Japanese birth certificate, but it's really a family registry. And my name on the registry is Sachiko plus Mommy's maiden name of Yamada. That's the name that's on my Japanese passport."

"But you're no longer a Japanese citizen."

"No, but my passport doesn't expire for another year. Anyway, when I heard that KKT, the leftist television station, was coming to Vietnam, to Cam Ranh, and needed a translator, I applied using my Japanese name. There's no way they would have hired a *gaijin*, especially an American. So that's why I had the accent and the name."

"You're pretty good at deception, aren't you."

"Well," she smiled, "after all, I *am* an attorney."

We laughed some more. Then I got serious.

"Sam, it's dangerous here."

"I know, but *you're* here. And I just *had* to see you. And besides, the man I love says everything is fated to be, anyway."

We made love again, slower this time. We wanted to savor every moment, cherish the experience.

And then it was time for me to leave. We shared a long, passionate kiss, and I left.

As I walked back to my ward, I realized how anxious I was for Sam to leave the danger of Vietnam. And, for the first time in my life, I knew what it felt like to really worry about someone I loved.

19

August 15, 1969

I was really ready to get back flying. The whole time at Cam Ranh, I had been concerned that I might be medically grounded, and the doctors at the Cam Ranh hospital couldn't shed any light on my flight status.

When it was time to leave the hospital, the orderly handed me a pristine set of camouflaged fatigues and a new pair of jungle boots. I put on the fatigues and laced up the boots. It was a shame my old boots had gotten lost somewhere along the way. They were broken in and comfortable. The new boots seemed stiff, and would require a long break-in period to make them feel right. As I glanced into the mirror in the latrine, it hit me. I looked like an FNG!

The C-9 flight from Cam Ranh to DaNang was markedly different from the one from NKP. The first flight, going to Cam Ranh, had been full of wounded and injured on their way

117

to the hospital. This flight had fewer passengers, and all of us were ambulatory, in relatively good condition. We were on our way back to our operational units. No one was on a stretcher. We were all in airline-type seats.

When I arrived at DaNang, there was an ambulance waiting planeside to take me to the DaNang hospital. When I got to the hospital, I was escorted to the Flight Surgeon's office.

The Flight Surgeon was a young Captain, probably not much older than me. The name plate on his desk read, "Captain Richard Ross, M.D."

"Hi, Hamilton, I'm Doctor Ross. I understand you're anxious to get back on flying status."

"I sure am."

"How are you feeling?"

"I feel great." I really wanted to tell him that I'd been healthy enough to have sex less than a week ago, but I thought better of it.

"Let me take a look at your wound."

I lowered my pants and showed the scar to the doctor.

"Have you tried sitting for any length of time?"

"Yes. No problems."

"What is the duration of your typical sortie?"

"Sometimes they can last five hours, usually four."

"Okay, if you tell me you can sit for five hours, and if you're no longer taking pain meds, you're cleared to fly again."

"That's affirmative. No pain meds, no problem sitting.

"Okay," he said, as he signed my flight clearance, "you're good to go."

"Thank you, doc."

As I was leaving the Flight Surgeon's office, I passed an open doorway to one of the wards in the hospital, and heard someone call out.

"Hey, Hamfist!"

It was Balls Balser, lying in one of the beds near the door. He looked terrible.

"What happened to you?" I asked.

"I got impaled on a piece of rebar during a rocket attack."

"A piece of what?"

"A piece of rebar, you know, the one-inch thick rods they use for forming concrete. Well, I was driving the Covey jeep to the hooch with an FNG when a rocket attack occurred. We could see the rockets hit. The first one landed in a field about 300 meters from us. The next one landed about 150 meters from us. We could tell the next one was going to get us, and we both bailed out of the jeep into the drainage ditch next to the road. It was a damn good thing we did, because the rocket was a direct hit on our jeep."

"So what's the deal with the rebar?"

"Well, they were going to line the drainage ditch with concrete, and they had rebar everywhere, and I got skewered. I was totally stuck, with the fucking rebar going completely through me, in my stomach, out my back. Missed every vital organ, but I was stuck there like a butterfly on a pin board. Damn good thing the FNG was with me to go get help."

"How are you feeling right now?"

"I'm a little sore, but otherwise, I'm okay. The really shitty part is, I won't get a Champagne Flight. They're going to air-evac me back to the States tomorrow. And get this – I don't even get a fucking Purple Heart out of this. Can you believe that? They said it's not direct enemy action."

"Man, that really sucks. And I'm sorry to see you go, Balls."

"Well, I was going to DEROS in another

couple of weeks anyway. How about you? I heard you were hurt."

"Nothing too bad. I got shot in the ass, and had to stick around the Cam Ranh hospital until they were sure there was no infection. I'll try to come by tomorrow morning to say goodbye before you leave."

"Okay. See you tomorrow."

I thought it was a shit deal about Balls not getting a Purple Heart. Not that it meant that much. As Royce said, "A Purple Heart and ten cents will get you a cup of coffee at the BX cafeteria." Still, it wasn't right.

I hurried back to the squadron with my medical clearance, and knocked on the Ops Officer's open door.

Major Walters looked up from his desk, and his face brightened.

"Hamfist! Get your ass in here!"

He stood up and gave me a sincere hug.

"I'm really glad you're okay. You are feeling okay, aren't you?"

I nodded.

He motioned for me to take a seat.

"I'm ready to get back flying, sir."

"We need to talk about that, Hamfist."

"What do you mean, sir?"

"None of the FANs want to fly with you. They say it's nothing personal, but they feel like you're a magnet-ass."

"So, where does that leave me?"

"Look, Hamfist, you're a damn good FAC. We need you. I told the schedulers to only put you on solo day missions. How's that sit with you?"

Actually, it sat pretty well. I liked flying in the daytime. The only drawback was it was almost impossible to see ground fire in the daytime. Plus, of course, if I had to bail out again, there would be ten thousand gomers watching me descend in my parachute.

"I'm okay with that, sir."

"Also, I'd like to get you checked out as an FCF pilot."

"That's great!"

I'd been requesting a checkout as a Functional Check Flight pilot for several months. Whenever an aircraft underwent any maintenance other than minor servicing, it required an FCF.

A typical FCF mission lasted about an hour, and most of the FCF pilots flew six or seven flights on the days they performed FCF duty.

And the FCF pilots still performed FAC duties also. So, I'd be getting more flying, and more variety. And, as a Lieutenant, more flying was almost as good as more money. I was pumped.

"I've got to tell you one more thing, Hamfist."

"What's that?"

"Seventh Air Force said that if you get shot down again, your tour is over. No exceptions."

"I understand."

I didn't really agree, but I understood. Not that it would change the way I operated. Not one iota.

"So, are you ready to start flying?"

"Absolutely."

"Good. I have you on the schedule to get your FCF checkout this afternoon. You'll be flying with Lieutenant Dover. One of the Pleiku birds sustained heavy damage. It got repaired here, and needs an FCF, then you can both ferry the airplane back to Pleiku. You can catch the Klong back here after the delivery."

The Klong was the C-130 that made cargo runs all over Southeast Asia.

I always got a kick out of the way Major Walters couldn't call Ben Dover by his name, it was always "Lieutenant Dover". Ben was the only Covey who didn't have a nickname. We called him by his real name.

Ben had arrived at DaNang a few months after me. When Major Walters saw the name "Benjamin Dover", he held an informal, impromptu squadron meeting to see what name we should assign to Dover.

Someone suggested the name "Work". I suggested "Fuck". When I shouted it out, Major Walters gave me a dirty look. Finally, we generally agreed we should just let him use his own name, Ben.

A month or so after Ben arrived, he and I were drinking in the Doom Club bar. I'd had a few drinks, and finally got up the nerve to ask him about his name.

"Hey, Ben, did your parents have some twisted sense of humor when they named you?"

"Everyone asks me that. My parents were French Jews who came to America right after World War II, right before I was born. The family name was D-e-a-u-v-e-u-r. When they processed through Immigration, the officer suggested they Americanize the name by spelling it D-o-v-e-r. Jewish tradition is to name children after a deceased relative. I was named after my grandfather, Benjamin. He died in the Holocaust. My parents never thought anything about the way it would sound in English."

Before I left Major Walter's office, I asked, "Can I ask a favor? Would it be possible for me to get a two-day CTO and catch the Klong from Pleiku to NKP? I'd really like to meet up with the guys who saved my ass."

Every few months, we would get Compensatory Time Off for a few days. It was a way to pay us back for the months of working with no days off. A lot of guys would go to nice, peaceful areas of Vietnam, such as Vung Tau or Cam Ranh Bay. Obviously, Cam Ranh Bay was not so peaceful any more. Sometimes, guys would go to Thailand, either Ubon or NKP. They called it "getting their horns trimmed". So basically, a CTO was an in-country or out-of-country R&R.

"No problem. I'll get some orders cut right away."

"Thank you, sir."

I made a quick trip back to the hospital to tell Balls I wouldn't be around for his departure, and we said our goodbyes right there.

G. E. Nolly

20

August 15, 1969

Before I went to fly the FCF, I went by the Armory desk of the Life Support Section. I needed to get a new Smith & Wesson pistol and a new AR-15, and I wanted to have extra magazines for the AR-15. Sergeant Wilson, the NCO In Charge of the Life Support Section, was behind the desk.

"Lieutenant Hancock," he said, "Welcome back, sir. I have some paperwork for you to fill out."

"No problem, Sarge. Where do I sign?"

I knew there would be paperwork to account for property lost in combat. I just hadn't realized how *much* paperwork there would be. Form after form. In duplicate or triplicate.

"I'm surprised I don't have to fill out a form for the missing airplane."

"I guess that will be between you and the Squadron Commander, sir."

"Okay. I'll take care of that with the squadron. Next order of business, I need four extra magazines for the AR."

"Four? Lieutenant, are you planning on carrying out a pitched battle?"

"I hope not, but I don't plan on running out of ammunition again. Also, I need a karabiner, to hook my AR to my survival vest."

Sergeant Wilson rustled through a drawer for a few seconds, and then produced a large snap link.

"Will this do, sir?"

"Perfect."

I had lost my AR-15 when I bailed out, and didn't want that to happen again. If I snapped the rifle to my survival vest, right at the top, along the shoulder, I would have it with me if I ever had to bail out again.

Senior Airman Davis walked into the Life Support section just as I was about to leave. He had the appearance of a young Muhammad Ali. He was African-American, about twenty years old, and probably six foot two, 220 pounds.

His face lit up as soon as he saw me.

"Lieutenant Hancock! It's great to see you, sir! I've been praying for you every day you were gone."

He started to try to hug me, then, thinking better of it, held out his hand. I could tell he had been genuinely worried about me.

"Thank you, Airman Davis. I'm sure it helped."

"See," I said, turning around, "no worse for wear."

"I hear that, sir."

Senior Airman Davis was a really friendly, if not terribly military, airman. He always had a big smile. And his uniform always looked messy.

As I left the Life Support section, I could hear Sergeant Wilson starting in on him.

"Davis, straighten your gig line! And don't slouch!"

I walked out to the Pleiku bird to meet up with Ben.

Although Ben had arrived in Vietnam after me, he had been assigned FCF duty months ago. He had worked his way through college as an Airframe and Powerplant mechanic, working on airplanes, and he was a perfect selection for FCF duty. He really knew his stuff, and gave me a very thorough briefing on FCF duties and responsibilities.

Basically, during an FCF my job was to

check every major aircraft system, including weapons release. There was a detailed checklist specifying all the actions that needed to be accomplished on the flight. It was perfect training for a pilot who wanted to ultimately become a test pilot. If I ever got offered an assignment to Test Pilot School, at Edwards Air Force Base, I sure wouldn't turn it down.

While a normal preflight check would take about five minutes, an FCF preflight could stretch to 30 minutes or longer. Ben explained everything to me as we performed the checks. I could see that he was very meticulous, a real perfectionist.

We performed all of our systems checks on the way down to Pleiku. Then we decided to do a little sightseeing. I had never been to Pleiku before, but Ben had delivered several airplanes there.

"Take a look over there," he said, pointing out his window, "I'm getting a woodie just looking at it."

"What's that?"

"Over there," he said, "that's Pussy Mountain."

I looked in the direction he was pointing, and I couldn't believe what I saw. If there was ever an appropriately-named landmark, it was Pussy Mountain.

It looked a lot, no, *precisely*, like a *mons pubis*.

"Is that a natural formation?" I asked. As soon as I asked the question, I realized how stupid it was. This thing was so gigantic, it couldn't have been man-made. It was just a gigantic perfect pubic mound, either natural or created by aliens with a really great sense of humor.

We landed at Pleiku, and I headed over to the FAC squadron to visit with the Pleiku Covey FACs while I waited for the Klong. While I was there, I filled everyone in on Willy Wilson's condition. I ran into Moose and related to him how much Willy had appreciated him saving his life. Moose definitely needed to be recommended for an Airman's Medal.

After a short visit, it was time for me to get on the C-130. There was a Pleiku Covey also hitching a ride to NKP. We were the only passengers.

We introduced ourselves to the C-130 crew, and the Aircraft Commander invited us to sit on the jump seat in the cockpit.

"We only have one headset, though," he

explained. "One of you can listen in on the headset for the first half of the flight, and then you can trade."

Good deal. I'd never been in the cockpit of a crew aircraft, and I looked forward to listening in on the way they ran their checklists.

It was getting dark as the C-130 crew went through their preflight procedures and started the four engines. I found it interesting, but once we were airborne, it was pretty boring, and I handed the headset to the Pleiku Covey. I quickly fell asleep in the jump seat.

I was awakened by the ringing of a loud bell. I sat up with a start, and looked around the cockpit. It was empty, and a red light was flashing. I jumped up and looked back into the cargo compartment, and saw the crew, all three C-130 crewmembers plus the Pleiku Covey, running to the open tailgate of the airplane, frantically donning their parachutes.

I looked around the cockpit for a parachute. None. I looked in the cargo compartment. No more parachutes.

As I started becoming frantic, they all walked back up to the cockpit, laughing hysterically. The airplane had been on autopilot, and the joke they had played on me had made their day. I had to admit, it was pretty damn funny.

When I got to NKP, I immediately headed to the SAR squadron. No one was there, because it was already pretty late. I remembered how to get to Vince's hooch, and I went there.

When I entered, Vince looked like he'd seen a ghost. He gave me a huge hug, and then he took me around the hooch and introduced me to the Spad pilots who had rescued me. We all went to the bar, and I bought all the drinks.

I had a really great visit with Vince and the guys, and then Vince and I looked up Don Springer. Don was my classmate at Laughlin and had gone to the Academy with Vince and me. He was now a Nail FAC based at NKP.

"I heard you've had an interesting tour," Don said, after we greeted.

"Well," I responded, "I could tell you a bunch of war stories. But you know the difference between a war story and a fairy tale, right?"

"Yeah, one begins 'Once upon a time', the other begins 'This is no shit'. After that, there's no difference."

"Bingo!"

Don, Vince and I went off base and had dinner at a really nice Thai restaurant, then I spent the night at Vince's hooch. We stayed up late swapping stories.

We all spent some time together the next day, until a klaxon sounded and both Vince and Don had to go fly. I closed my eyes and said a silent prayer, hoping that the Hamfist curse had been defeated.

I caught the Klong back to DaNang that night.

It had been a good visit.

21

August 17, 1969

It was time for Major Walters to DEROS, and a replacement Ops Officer had not yet even been identified by the Military Personnel Center, let alone arrived. As a Major, Scooter Scoville became our new Ops Officer.

Fish was scheduled to DEROS next month, and had been on pins and needles for weeks, waiting for his assignment. He had designated F-4s to Lakenheath Air Base, in England, on his "dream sheet". Since all of us who volunteered for Vietnam were promised our choice of assignments, it was a foregone conclusion that Fish would be going to England. But still, he fidgeted.

I was in our room, writing a letter to Sam, when Fish stormed in, pissed. Really pissed.

"I can't believe this shit. They *promised* me my choice of airplanes! They promised!"

"What happened? What did you get?"

" A fucking B-52! I'm not going to go to training. Fuck them!"

"Fish, you gotta go where they send you."

"What the fuck are they going to do? Send me to Vietnam?"

"Have you talked to the Ops Officer, or the Squadron Commander?"

"Yeah. Scooter is the one who told me. He said it was needs of the service. What bullshit!"

I had never seen him so angry. Then, suddenly, he calmed down.

"I know what I'm going to do. I'm going to prove to them it wouldn't make financial sense to send me to buffs."

"How are you going to do that?"

"Well, you know I have a Date of Separation, a DOS, ten months after my DEROS. That way I won't get a four-year service commitment for B-52 training. It costs a lot of money, probably over a half-million dollars, to train a B-52 copilot. Training takes six months. There's *no way* they would pay that kind of money to train me if they're only going to get four months of use out of me."

"Wait a minute. I thought you wanted F-4s. Training for the F-4 is six months also. Why would they send you to F-4s if they would only get four more months out of you?"

"If I got F-4s I was going to pull my DOS. Now all I want to do is instruct in the O-2 at Hurlburt and get the fuck out of the Air Force on my DOS. This is bullshit!"

True to his word, Fish wrote a very detailed, compelling Staff Study demonstrating that it was not economically feasible to send him to B-52 training if SAC would only get a few months of utilization out of him. He even went to the Personnel Office and found out how much it cost to train a B-52 copilot. It was close to $700,000. He made a good case.

About a week after he mailed the Staff Study to Strategic Air Command Headquarters, Fish got a response: we'll accept the cost, you're not getting out of B-52s, mother-fucker.

To make matters worse, about two weeks later, Fish got his base assignment. He was assigned to Minot Air Force Base, in upstate North Dakota. It seemed SAC had a ton of northern-tier bases, all in frigid, out-of-the-way locations.

Fish had been fucked, and all of us worried that we'd get fucked, also.

Fish was morose and sullen the rest of his time at DaNang, all the way up to his DEROS.

He just wasn't the same guy who had been so bubbly and enthusiastic when he'd returned from R&R in Sydney.

At his going-away party, Fish made the shortest farewell speech in squadron history.

He stood up and said, "You know how to tell when an Air Force Personnel Officer is lying? When his lips are moving." Then he sat down.

It was grim.

After Fish DEROSed, I didn't have a room-mate for a few weeks. Then a few FNGs arrived, and one of them, Beaver Beemis, became my new room-mate.

He looked so young, and so green! Was that what I looked like last January? Did I want to even tell Beaver any of my stories? I was an old head now, and I wanted to give him words of wisdom. But I didn't want to scare the shit out of him. I decided to hold off on the war stories until I thought he could handle them.

One of our pilots, we called him Numb-nuts, but his official handle was Coonass, came back one day with rice all over the belly of his aircraft, and the rear propeller bent forward. He tried to pass it off as enemy action, but it was obvious he'd been fucking around. It turned out he liked to do acrobatics, even though acrobatics were prohibited in the O-2. Apparently he tried to perform a low-altitude loop over a rice paddy. He almost made it.

When he hit the rice paddy, instead of crashing, the airplane bounced. But he had been pulling on the yoke so hard, the aircraft had been in an extreme nose-up attitude, and the rear prop hit the ground during the bounce.

His penance was to assist the mechanics in the repair of the airplane. And he was "promoted" to the staff position of Group Safety Officer.

"Now that," said Miles Miller, "is a perfect example of Fuck Up And Move Up."

"What do you mean," I asked.

"He fucked up, they put him in a staff job where he'll get a lot of visibility, and he'll probably make Major below the zone. Fuck Up And Move Up."

22

August 30, 1969

Scooter Scoville called me into his office before my flight.

"I have some good news for you, Hamfist."

"What's that, sir?

"Seventh Air Force just notified me that the area where you were shot down is going to be bombarded with an Arc Light attack today. TOT of 2330 zulu."

I did a quick mental calculation. I would be airborne and in the AO at 2330.

"That's great news, sir. It's a shame we won't be able to get any BDA."

"Well, if you've ever seen an Arc Light, you know it's sure going to ruin their day."

I thought back to my first day in Vietnam, when we all climbed to the roof of the Covey hooch to watch a B-52 raid near DaNang. Yeah, it was sure going to ruin their day.

I couldn't wait to get airborne. I flew to the AO and checked the time. At 2320 zulu, there was a Heavy Artillery Warning transmitted on Guard, with the area coordinates. When it was 2325 zulu, I flew over to the area where I had been shot down. I rolled in and fired a couple of willie petes about two klicks – kilometers – away, then I made a hasty retreat to get as far away from the target as I could. I looked up and saw the line of B-52s approaching, high above.

I figured the gomers were probably just like us – they probably wanted to watch an airstrike. Just like the way we all got on the roof of the Covey hooch to watch the Arc Light on New Year's Day. With the willie petes a few klicks away, they would probably think the attack was going to be in that location, and they would come out of hiding and try to watch the show. And they would be totally exposed during the Arc Light.

I was already about ten miles away when the bombs hit, and it was awe-inspiring. And I really felt good to see those bastards getting blown to kingdom come.

During the Arc Light I had set up a figure-8 holding pattern well away from the route structure, just some nondescript location over the jungle, where I wouldn't need to worry about ground fire and could watch the show. But I was still flying my airplane, and still looking around.

Just as the Arc Light finished, as I was making a left turn, I glanced down at the jungle under the left wing of my aircraft. At that very moment, the triple-canopy jungle opened up, just for a second, probably due to a gust of wind. And, there, directly beneath my aircraft, I saw a SAR letter, made from a signal panel. As the jungle closed, it was gone as quickly as it had appeared.

The signal panel in our survival vest was a large rectangular piece of orange nylon, that could be used to attract an aircraft's attention. It could also be easily torn into pieces to create a SAR letter.

Each month, the SAR letter would change. This letter on the ground was the letter "V". I checked my frequency card and saw that V was the letter from October. So whoever had put that letter on the ground had been shot down last October.

Was it possible there a fellow aviator down there, still trying to get rescued? Could somebody evade and survive in the jungle for all these months? Of course it was possible – weren't they still finding Japanese soldiers in the Philippines, all these years after the war? If he's using his signal panel, he probably doesn't have his survival radio any more. I was probably his only hope.

I immediately thought of Major Swain.

23

August 30, 1969

Major Griffin "Griff" Swain was my Air Officer Commanding at the Academy. The AOC's job was to be in charge of one of the 24 cadet squadrons, about 100 cadets each. An AOC assignment was considered choice duty, and the Academy was highly selective in assigning officers to AOC positions.

Major Swain was a terrific role model for our squadron, Cadet Squadron 11. He was a former fighter pilot, and, because he wasn't a graduate of a service academy himself, he always went the extra mile to connect with the cadets.

An example was the PFT. As cadets, we had to take the Physical Fitness Test, either once or twice each year. The test consisted of five events: pull-ups, pushups, standing broad jump, sit-ups, and 600-yard run. Each event was scored, with a maximum score of 100 points for each event. I was always able to get

100 points for 18 pull-ups, 100 points for 60 pushups, 100 points for 100 sit-ups in 2 minutes, and 100 points for standing broad-jump. But I never could run the 600 yards in a minute and a half to get 100 points, so the best score I ever got was a 490. Anyone who got a score of 400 or better only had to take the PFT once a year. Cadets who got less than 400 had to take it every semester. Anyone who got a 500 never had to take it again, his entire time at the Academy. That didn't happen very often.

Major Swain participated in the PFT with the 11th Squadron cadets, even though AOCs were not required to take the PFT. In fact, only one other AOC ever took the PFT, a Marine Exchange Officer. But there was a difference. Major Swain scored a 500! And he was no spring chicken, probably 33 or 34 years old.

When I was a new cadet, Major Swain invited several of us doolies to his home for lunch one weekend. For a doolie, having a home-cooked meal was a really big deal. After lunch, Major Swain drove us to Seven Falls, a local Colorado Springs landmark. We climbed the steps to the top of the seven waterfalls, and then we all hiked about a mile thro intough the forest. At the end of the trail we came to a clearing that spread out for several yards, ending with a cliff. The view was magnificent.

"See that monument? This is where Katherine Lee Bates stood when she was inspired to write 'America The Beautiful'. Some people think she got her inspiration from the top of Pikes Peak, but this was the actual spot."

Major Swain was a real inspiration to all of us, a real leader. When I was in the hospital after my appendectomy, he came by to visit me. I was shocked. The entire cadet wing had traveled to Chicago for the inaugural Army-Air Force football game, and the AOCs traveled with the squadrons. I had assumed he had gone with 11th Squadron.

"Sir! Why aren't you in Chicago?" I asked.

He calmly responded, "Cadet Hancock, our cadets have all the adult supervision they need. You're a member of our squadron, and I don't go on a good deal trip until and unless everyone in the squadron goes."

"Besides," he added, "President Kennedy had to miss the game also, so we're in good company."

"The President didn't attend?"

"No, he canceled. There was an assassination of the brothers Diem and Nhu in Vietnam. There were all kinds of meetings as a result of the assassinations that took priority."

"Where's Vietnam?"

I had heard of Vietnam, but, to me in 1963, it was just some faraway, insignificant country. To me, it seemed a lot like the islands of Quemoy and Matsu, which had been such a hot-button issue a year earlier, then disappeared from the headlines. Surely, I'd thought, whatever was going on there would fade away in another year or so.

"It's in Southeast Asia. One of these days it might be important."

After he finished his assignment at the Academy, Major Swain was assigned to fly RF-4s. He didn't return from a mission over Laos the day after my graduation from pilot training, last October. It put a pall over my last days at Laughlin.

Was it possible the SAR letter was placed there by Major Swain?

I tried to keep the exact location in sight as I made a sweeping turn to the left. I didn't want to fly directly over the location again, for fear of compromising the survivor's position. I tried to look around and see if I could find any prominent landmarks that would point my eyes back to the SAR letter.

I checked my position with the TACAN, the onboard navigation system. I got a rough radial and DME from Ubon, but it was only a very basic position. It could be as much as five miles away from the actual position. I dug out 1-to-50 charts from my map bag, to try to determine the exact position. I kept trying to figure out where I was, while trying to keep the survivor's position in sight.

And then, somehow, I lost sight of the SAR letter's location.

I don't know exactly how it happened, but it happened. The jungle was extremely rugged terrain, and there were no roads for miles. The only way to determine a position was by reading contour lines on the map. And I was really bad at visualizing terrain by looking at contour lines. I was supposed to have received additional instruction in map reading at FAC-U, but our training had been cut short whan Mitch went and we'd all been shipped off to snake school .

Some guys were really good at reading contour lines. The Army Huey pilots were expert at it. They flew Nap of the Earth – NOE – for a living. They didn't need roads to figure out where they were. They were eighteen, nineteen year old kids, enlisted guys, and they could read contour lines. I was twenty-three, an officer, and I was a failure at the most basic function of being a FAC.

I heard Covey 245, Potts Potter, check in on Hillsboro frequency. Potts was in an OV-10. I came up on Hillsboro frequency.

"Covey 245, Covey 218. I need to talk to you on secure fox mike."

"Roger, coming over."

We almost never used secure FM. We always had the capability, using the KY-28 COMSEC equipment on board, but normally it was used for air-to-ground communications with ground commanders, to ensure the gomers wouldn't know what was being said. Since we never worked Troops-In-Contact – TIC – over the trail, we didn't have any need to actually use the KY-28. We tested it on every flight with a radio check with Ops, but never needed it in operations. Until now.

I channelized the KY-28 and made a call in the blind.

"Covey 218 standing by on fox mike."

"Covey 245 here. What's up, Hamfist?"

"I'm at the 086 for 117 off the Ubon TACAN, at 5000 feet, and I saw a SAR letter in this vicinity. Now I can't find it again."

"What are you doing over there?"

"Long story. Will you help me look for the letter?"

"Sure. I'll be there in about ten."

The OV-10 was the perfect airplane to help me. It could fly slow if it needed, could go fast, and had lots of power, so Cover 245 would be able to make a low pass over the area and quickly climb back to altitude. It would take me six or seven minutes to get back up to altitude if I made a low pass.

Covey 245 showed up sooner than I expected, and made numerous passes over the area, much lower than I could have safely flown. We hung around there for over an hour, and never heard anyone come up on the radio, never saw a mirror flash, never saw anything.

I was sure there was a survivor down there, maybe Major Swain, clinging to life. I could imagine how ecstatic he must have been, seeing me fly overhead and enter a left orbit. He was counting on me for his very survival.

And I let him down.

24

August 30, 1969

After I landed, I felt like a total failure. I was incompetent at the most fundamental piloting skill. I tried to rationalize it. I hadn't received enough instruction. All of my missions had been over the route structure, so there was no need to read contour lines except to determine spot target elevations for the fighters. Almost all of my flying had been at night, when I couldn't see the terrain, anyway.

The rationalizing didn't work. Any other FAC in the same situation would have gotten a good plot. Then Snake and his team could have been inserted, maybe rescued the survivor. As it was, the survivor would likely die, and it would be my fault.

How the hell could I have called myself a FAC? I was just a goddam airplane driver, a little, dinky airplane at that. I'm lucky they're letting me fly FCFs.

I needed to hear Sam's voice. I went to the MARS station, waited my turn, and placed the call. She could immediately tell that something was wrong.

"What's wrong, Ham? I can hear it in your voice. Over."

"I can't discuss it on the phone, but I made a serious mistake today, and I feel terrible. Over."

"Ham, you're human. I'm human. We all make mistakes. Don't be too hard on yourself. Over."

If it had been any other time, I would have come back with some smart-ass reply, like, "You can't say hard-on over the radio." Instead, I remained silent.

"Ham, are you there? Over."

"Yes, I'm here, Sam. I just really needed to hear your voice. I love you, Sam. Goodbye. Over."

I took off the headset and left the MARS station before I even heard her response.

25

September 23, 1969

I'd been flying FCFs almost exclusively. At least I couldn't hurt anyone else on an FCF mission.

As a break from FCF flying, I was assigned to carry an Army Green Beret Major on a local flight to survey an island a few miles off the coast of China Beach. His unit had inserted a recon team onto the island about a week before, and he had lost contact with them.

"Hello, sir, I'm Hamfist Hancock."

"I'm Rusty Warner," he said, returning my salute and then shaking my hand. "Thanks for taking me up today."

"Glad to help, sir."

"I inserted a team on Cat Island almost a week ago, and I haven't been able to make radio contact with them for several days. I'd like to fly over the island and see if they come up on the radio or give me a mirror flash or some other kind of signal."

"Okay, sir. Climb aboard."

We took off and headed out to the west, then turned south for about a mile.

"There it is. Cat Island," Major Warner said, pointing ahead and to the left.

From Major Warner's description, I had expected a much larger island. This island was small, extremely small. Maybe 300 yards long and 100 yards wide. About the size of the Academy stadium, including the seats. It was inconceivable to me that a team of men could just disappear in there.

We flew over the island at about 1000 feet, and I gunned the engines a few times. We hung around for about an hour.

No response.

"Where to now, sir?"

"Can you take me to Phu Bai?"

"Sure. No problem."

I headed north to Phu Bai. It was located next to the walled city of Hue, not far from the DMZ. It was really fun to go to another base, since almost all of my flying had been out of DaNang.

Unlike DaNang's long, hard surface

runways, Phu Bai had a much shorter PSP runway. PSP was perforated steel planking, and had the surface friction of an ice skating rink when it was wet. I'd only landed on PSP one other time, when I'd flown a short mission to Marble Mountain, a few miles south of DaNang.

We landed at Phu Bai, taxied to the ramp, and Major Warner and I deplaned.

"I need to visit one of my units for a few minutes," he said, as we approached a tent, "Come on in."

We entered the tent and Major Warner introduced me to a few Green Beret officers, a Captain and two Lieutenants. They showed me around, and I was immediately struck by how good we had it in the Air Force. This was the Army. The only furniture in the tent was an austere green wooden table, a few folding chairs, and a coffee pot sitting next to some styrofoam cups.

While Major Warner discussed some operational issues with his officers, I poured myself a cup of coffee and cooled my heels. After about fifteen minutes, we headed back to the airplane. I couldn't help but notice the weapons Major Warner had.

"Sir, what kind of sidearm is that? Is it a

machine pistol?"

"Not exactly. It's an Uzi, fully automatic, made in Israel. It uses 9 millimeter ammunition, just like my pistol," he answered, holding up his Browning Hi-Power semi-auto. "I only need to carry one kind of ammo."

"Why is it better than an M-16? Does it have a higher rate of fire?"

"No. Actually, it has a much slower rate of fire. The M-16 fires way too fast, and you can't walk your rounds to the target because you go through the entire magazine too quickly. That's why I like the Uzi."

"How many rounds does the Browning carry?"

"Thirteen rounds in the magazine, and one in the chamber."

"Wow. That's the kind of firepower I wish I'd had when I was down in the jungle in Laos."

"Well, it's hard to get a hold of these. But I'll tell you what. When I leave Vietnam, you can have them."

"Really? That's great! Thank you, sir. When's your DEROS?"

"April."

"Oh. I DEROS in December."

"Sorry."

We flew back to DaNang, and Major Warner promised me if he heard about any Uzi and Browning Hi-Powers, he'd let me know.

When I got back to the squadron, Scooter asked me if I would fly an FCF.

"Sure. No problem."

"Just watch the weather. Make sure you stay VMC when you do your checks. There's a front moving in. You may have to get a few miles feet wet before you get in the clear."

Feet wet meant being out over the ocean.

"One other thing," he added, "did you know a former Covey named Buzz Watson?"

"The war lover? Yeah, I met him right before he left to fly as a Raven. Why?"

"We just got a report that he's MIA. He was on a Raven mission with a Laotian observer, and they didn't come back."

I thought back to my first conversation with Buzz. He was the first person to discuss fatalism with me. During that conversation, Buzz had told me how he wanted to die, if it ever came to it. Just like Buzz had said, he was doing something he loved, something that began with the letter F.

Flying an FCF required total concentration,

and I was happy for the diversion from the deep funk I was in when I wasn't flying. Some days I flew six FCFs, logging almost eight hours of flying time. Maybe if I got more flying time, I wouldn't be so fucking incompetent.

The weather was beginning to turn sour as I took off on the FCF. At about 400 feet on takeoff, I entered the clouds. I immediately turned to the east to head out over the water, climbing out on instruments. I held rock-steady on a heading of 090.

I enjoyed flying on instruments. We didn't have an opportunity to do it very often, but I had always been a good instrument pilot in pilot training, and being on instruments made me feel like a real pilot.

For some reason, I don't know why, I looked out ahead of the aircraft. There was no reason to look outside the aircraft, since I was in solid instrument conditions. But I looked out anyway.

And suddenly, all I could see directly ahead of my aircraft, rushing at me at 120 knots, was triple-canopy jungle. I instinctively pulled up and performed the box canyon maneuver.

I had read about the maneuver in a flying magazine when I was in pilot training. It was a way of getting out of a box canyon, a canyon with gradually rising terrain that wasn't wide enough to perform a level turn.

To execute the maneuver, the pilot had to sharply pull the aircraft up into a steep climb and unload to zero-Gs. If the aircraft wasn't unloaded, it would stall. For an aircraft to stall it had to exceed the critical angle of attack. It wouldn't do that if there was no G-loading.

Once unloaded in a zero-G condition, the pilot had to put in full rudder to get the nose to come around. The aircraft would then be in a steep nose-low attitude, accelerating in the opposite direction. It was really important to keep the airplane unloaded, or it would enter a spin. Not good close to the ground.

I had practiced the maneuver numerous times, just for fun, in the O-2. I had never really expected to need to use it, I was just practicing it for something to do when I was bored during daytime missions when I couldn't find any targets.

Now it was for real. I pulled hard on the yoke until the aircraft was about 50 degrees nose up. The airspeed dropped off precipitously, and I pushed forward to totally unload to zero-G. I stuffed in right rudder, and watched the nose swing down to 30 degrees nose low. I was flying again, and hadn't crashed into the trees. Now I had to figure out what the hell had happened.

I had been flying on a heading of east. There's nothing but the South China Sea east of DaNang. This just didn't compute. My heading indicator now read 270, due west.

Then I checked my standby "whiskey" compass. It read 180. I immediately knew what had happened. My heading indicator, which was a gyro instrument, had precessed. When I had been flying on an indicated heading of east, I had been slowly turning to a heading of north. If I had been checking my turn-and-slip indicator, I would have noticed that I had been turning to the left. I had narrowly missed crashing into Monkey Mountain.

Monkey Mountain was on a peninsula northeast of DaNang. There was a Navy radar detachment at the top of the mountain, and several airplanes had reportedly crashed into the mountain over the years. I had almost joined them.

Now that I had analyzed the problem, I was able to continue flying, using the whiskey compass. It was named the whiskey compass because the compass card rotated in a liquid container mounted at the top of the windscreen. Back in the early days of aviation, the liquid was supposedly whiskey. In the O-2, the liquid was a chemical with about twenty letters in its name.

The liquid was highly corrosive and dangerous if its fumes were inhaled. A few months earlier, my whiskey compass had started leaking, and my FAN and I both started feeling dizzy. Fortunately, I had an airsickness barf-bag in my flight suit pocket, and took it out and tied it around the whiskey compass. Then we opened the windows and, after a few minutes, we felt okay.

I headed east and continued climbing, and finally got into the clear. I performed the FCF, then headed back toward DaNang. I made contact with DaNang Approach, and got vectored in for a GCA – Ground Controlled Approach.

As I was being vectored on downwind, in the clouds, my Attitude Indicator failed. The Attitude Indicator was powered by an inverter on the instrument rack behind the pilot seat. The inverter's job was to convert DC – direct current – to AC – alternating current, the type of electricity the Attitude Indicator needed for proper operation. The O-2 actually had two inverters, so I selected the INV toggle switch on the instrument panel to ALT and used the alternate inverter. The Attitude Indicator OFF flag went away for about 30 seconds, then came into view again.

I looked back over my shoulder at the instrument rack, and immediately saw the problem. The plexiglass window on the left aft side of the aircraft was not sealing well, and moisture from the cloud I was flying in was entering the aircraft through the leaky window. The location of the inverters on the instrument rack, right next to the window, was an unfortunate coincidence. Just when I needed my Attitude Indicator, when flying in instrument conditions, it failed due to water shorting out the inverters.

My radios were still working, and I advised Approach Control that I would need a gyro-out approach. Approach vectored me to the runway using "Turn now, stop turn" commands to guide me in. It was challenging, but rewarding when I finally broke out of instrument conditions and saw the runway.

Needless to say, I had a lot of aircraft discrepancies to report to maintenance.

When I arrived back at Ops after my FCF, there was a large sealed envelope with my name on it in my distribution box. It was stamped "Eyes Only", meaning it was only for my personal viewing.

I opened the envelope, and it was a rejection of my Extension Request. President Nixon had ordered troop withdrawals from Vietnam, and all extension requests were automatically cancelled. Without an extension, I couldn't become a Raven FAC.

It was just as well. The Ravens were the best of the best in the FAC world. At this point, I was certain I would never have qualified.

G. E. Nolly

26

October 3, 1969

I placed another MARS call to Sam. I really needed to apologize for being so miserable on my past several calls. It was selfish of me.

This would be my last call to her before she left for Officer Training School, and I wanted to make sure she hadn't caught my malaise.

"Hi Sam, are you excited about your upcoming school? Over."

"You sound a lot better, Ham. Yes, I'm really pumped. That's the term, right? Over."

"It sure is. Have you been getting ready? Over."

"I sure have. I've been running five miles every day, and I can do fifty pushups. Not girlie pushups from the knees, real pushups. Over."

"I'm so proud of you. I know you're going to make Distinguished Graduate. Over."

"I have to. I can't let you show me up. Over."

"I love you, Sam. Have a safe trip. Goodbye. Over."

"I love you, too. Goodbye. Over."

Thank God I'd been able to talk to Sam before she left.

It was going to be a tough couple of months until I could hear her voice again.

27

November 10, 1969

I was sitting in the Doom Club with a couple of the other Covey FACs. The weather had been especially lousy, with squall line thunderstorms over the mountains between DaNang and Laos. Because of the weather either over the target area or over our route to the AO, we hadn't flown any missions in several days. We were getting antsy, and spent most of our time bitching. And drinking.

We were about to order another round of drinks, when in walked a Marine Lieutenant. It was Lieutenant Royce!

"Who wants to help celebrate the Marine Corps birthday?" he bellowed. I got the impression he'd already started celebrating a bit earlier.

When he saw me, his eyes lit up.

"Lieutenant! Great to see you. I have a jeep outside, and I can take five of you."

"I'm ready!" I answered, "Let's go."

Three other guys joined me in piling into the jeep for a quick, albeit dangerous, drive to Camp DaNang, the Marine outpost. When we arrived we spilled out and went into the Marine Officer's Club.

The Marines didn't know how to live in luxury, but they sure knew how to throw a party. All the booze we could drink. All the food, great food, we could eat. Steak, lobster, shrimp. We had a ball.

Like every other time I got shit-faced drunk, I blacked out. I think I had a good time. Next thing I knew, someone was shaking me.

"Lieutenant. Wake up." It was Royce.

I felt like crap. I lifted my head and looked around. I was on a canvas cot.

"It's 0500 hours," Royce proclaimed, "Let's go for a run."

"I, I think I'll pass," I responded.

"Okay. If you want to wash up, here's a basin." He handed me an empty helmet.

All I could think was, "You gotta be shitting me."

I thanked Royce and hitched a ride back to DaNang. Damn, those Marines knew how to throw a party!

When I got back to the Covey Squadron, there was a note to see the Squadron Commander. I knocked on his door, entered, and saluted.

"Lieutenant Hancock reporting as ordered, sir."

Lieutenant Colonel White, the new Squadron Commander, returned my salute, then held out his hand.

"Congratulations, Hamfist. We have a citation to present to you. Squadron meeting at noon. Wear your 1505s."

"Yes, sir."

I saluted and left. I was puzzled. I hadn't worn my 1505s, the tan uniform, since arriving in Vietnam. I went back to my hooch and dug out my 1505s. They were filthy.

I went out into the hallway and flagged down one of our maids. I reached into my pocket, dug out a few *piasters*, and handed them to her.

"I need this washed and ironed right away."

"No problem, *Dai Uy*. Have tomorrow." The maids, for some reason, called everyone *Dai Uy*. It was the Vietnamese word for Captain. I didn't mind the promotion.

"No, I need now." I pointed at my watch.

"Need right away." There was my pidgin English again.

"No problem."

I watched the maid, and hung around her like a hawk until I was sure she would get right to it.

Fortunately, the washing machine was working again. For about a three-month period, the washer had been broken. The maids had used their alternate method of washing our clothes: they put the laundry into the urinals, and repeatedly flushed until they felt like the laundry was done.

As soon as the maids started using the urinals to do the laundry, we all started getting various kinds of skin rashes. When he found out about the rashes, the Flight Surgeon came to our hooch and disconnected the dryer. The maids then had to lay the laundry items out on the lawn and let the sun dry them. The ultraviolet rays from the sun, he explained, would kill the germs that were causing our rashes.

And he had been correct. The rashes subsided virtually as soon as he disabled the dryer. When we finally had the washer repaired, the Flight Surgeon allowed us to use the dryer again.

The maid washed my uniform, dried it, and carefully ironed it. When I put it on, it looked and felt way too big.

I showed up at the squadron a few minutes before noon. The Squadron Admin Officer called me up to the front of the meeting room, and I waited there until everyone had been seated.

Then the Admin Officer called the room to attention, and the Squadron Commander entered. This was obviously some kind of big deal.

"Attention to orders," the Admin Officer announced. Everyone stood up at attention.

"Citation to accompany the award of the Silver Star Medal," he continued.

"The President of the United States of America, authorized by Act of Congress July 9, 1918 (amended by an act of July 25, 1963), takes pleasure in presenting the Silver Star to First Lieutenant Hamilton H. Hancock, United States Air Force, for gallantry in connection with military operations against an opposing enemy as a Forward Air Controller directing fighter aircraft in Southeast Asia on 1 August, 1969. On that date, Lieutenant Hancock, in his capacity as a Forward Air Controller, directed fighter aircraft against certain heavily defended hostile positions. After directing these aircraft, his aircraft received a direct hit from hostile anti-aircraft fire which forced him to bail out. Upon reaching the ground, Lieutenant Hancock continued to direct tactical aircraft both to aid in effecting his own rescue, as well as destroy a truck park which he discovered during his 40 hours on the ground. By his gallantry and devotion to duty, Lieutenant Hancock has reflected great credit upon himself and the United States Air Force."

I was speechless, as I stood at attention and the Squadron Commander pinned the Silver Star Medal on my chest. Then he shook my hand and saluted me. He saluted me! I returned the salute and remained at attention. An Air Force photographer was snapping pictures continuously during the presentation.

And then the assembly was dismissed. Everyone in the squadron came up to me and congratulated me. Receiving recognition from my peers was an incredibly heady experience.

I'd had no idea that I had been submitted for an award. The Squadron Admin Officer took care of the Awards and Decorations function, and he hadn't given me any hints that this was coming down the pike. I was glad I didn't play poker against him.

For the first time in months, I was starting to feel good about myself. This was a great day.

Until three o'clock.

G. E. Nolly

28

November 11, 1969

At three o'clock, the Squadron Commander called me back into his office.

"Hamfist, I have some bad news for you. And I hate to give it to you on your special day. But I'm required to deliver this information to you as soon as it arrives. I know you had your heart set on getting a fighter for your next assignment."

I gulped. I had heard this once before.

"I'm sorry to tell you," he continued, "you've been assigned to Air Force Specialty Code 1025."

"What's an AFSC 1025?"

"It's a B-52 pilot."

"But, sir, I have it in writing. I am supposed to get my choice of assignments after this tour."

"I'm sorry, Hamfist. Needs of the service."

This was really starting to sound familiar. To

be honest, I wasn't totally surprised, based on Fish's experience. But I had held out hope after hope I wouldn't get the same treatment as Fish. When I thought about Fish, I realized how selfish I had been. When Fish got a B-52 assignment, it was a shame he didn't get his F-4, but it would also be a career-broadening experience to fly a big aircraft. When I got my B-52 assignment, all I could think of was that I'd been screwed.

The rest of the day was pretty much a blur. I sat around in my hooch, feeling sorry for myself. And then there was a knock on my door.

It was Jack Jackson. Jack was a Captain, and had flown B-52s before becoming an OV-10 FAC.

"Hamfist, sorry to hear the news. I know my way around Strategic Air Command, and I think I may be able to help you somewhat."

"I don't think anybody can help me."

"Well, I can't get you that fighter you want, but I can help you get the best assignment in SAC."

"What's that?"

"Every B-52 assignment is at a SAC base, except one. At Mather Air Force Base, the B-52 squadron is a tenant unit in an Air Training Command base. That means the guys at Mather don't have to put up with all the typical SAC bullshit. It's a totally different lifestyle from every other SAC base."

"How do I get an assignment to Mather?"

"I'll help you. Let's get down to business."

Jack helped me craft a really great, bullshit letter to SAC Headquarters, telling them how much I was looking forward to becoming part of the Team (capital T) to counter the Soviet Threat (another capital T). Jack put the words in my mouth, and I typed them on the paper. I sent the letter off to SAC Headquarters and received my assignment to Mather in less than a week. I thought back to the days of the pig pool.

The pig pool was a really immature activity we Academy cadets had participated in during our field trip around the continental United States, called the Zone of the Interior. The ZI Field Trip was conducted during the summer after our first year at the Academy. We spent about a week at every major Air Force command, SAC, TAC, AFSC, MATS, and we also spent a week on the aircraft carrier Yorktown and a week at the Army parachute jump school, at Fort Benning. The ZI field trip took up most of the summer.

At every base we visited, there would be a formal ball. The base would bring local girls in for blind dates with the cadets. We would line up in one room off to the side of the ballroom, and the girls would line up in another room. Then we'd enter the ballroom, and be matched up with whatever girl entered through the other door.

With about 600 cadets on the field trip, and an equal number of girls, there was a good chance that not all the girls would be beauty queens. So we each chipped in a dollar for the pig pool. The official pig pool was the 20 or so ugliest girls. Whoever got the ugliest girl, as judged by a majority of the cadets in the post-ball voting, would collect the $600. It was pretty nice compensation for spending an evening with an ugly girl. Everyone wanted to get either a beautiful girl or win the pig pool. And no one wanted to come in second place in the pig pool!

I had heard the story – maybe true, maybe not – that during a previous ZI field trip, the cadet who had won the pig pool at one of the bases found out that the girl who was his assigned date had also won *her* pig pool!

The way I saw it, getting a B-52 to Mather

was the Air Force pilot equivalent of getting the prettiest girl in the pig pool.

29

November 25, 1969

After I had reported the SAR letter to our Intel department, the report had filtered up to Seventh Air Force and, unbeknownst to me, they had sent an RF-4 over the area. The recce bird made numerous sweeps in the vicinity I had reported, and the photo-analysts identified what looked like my SAR letter.

Now they had an exact location, and a Special Operations Group team was sent in to see if they could find a survivor. The group was led by Snake.

An SOG team looking for a survivor is tricky business. They can't just call out "We're Americans, here to save you." The survivor would probably think it was gomers trying to flush him out. At the same time, if gomers thought there was a team in the area, they might try to give an indication they were a survivor, to try to get the team to reveal their location. A real cat and mouse game.

Snake and his team had been on the ground for about two days, and had located the SAR letter. It was constructed out of survival kit nylon, so it may well have been legitimate. But there was no survivor.

The indigenous team members were expert trackers, and they searched for any signs of life, to no avail. Whoever had made the SAR letter was no longer in the area. It was time for the team to extract.

I had just entered the AO when Hillsboro called me to alert me of an extraction with a possible TIC situation. I flew to the area, set up an orbit, and listened to fox mike radio.

"Covey, this is Pappa Foxtrot 1."

Pappa Foxtrot – Prairie Fire.

"Pappa Foxtrot 1, Covey 218, go ahead."

"We're right below you, NOW, heading west. We need immediate pickup. We have made contact, and the gomers are hot on our ass."

I looked around for the closest area that could be a landing zone for a helicopter. I found one a few hundred meters to the south. I checked with Hillsboro, and they already had two choppers inbound, ETA 10 minutes.

"Okay, Pappa Fox, can you change your

direction of travel to south?"

"Affirmative."

"Okay, I have an LZ picked out for you about 200 meters south of what I think is your location."

"We're moving out. The gomers are pretty close."

I switched over to VHF and called Hillsboro.

"Hillsboro, Covey 218, we need immediate air, rendezvous Ubon 090 for 117."

"We have Catnip flight coming to you, ETA 5 minutes. Strike frequency Bravo"

"Roger."

Back to fox mike.

"Pappa Fox, when you see fighters overhead, pop a smoke. Don't tell me the color until I ask you."

"Roger."

The fighters checked in on UHF strike frequency Bravo.

"Catnip flight, check."

"Two."

"Covey, Catnip flight, two fox fours, Mark 82 snake-eyes, at the rendezvous."

Snake-eyes were high-drag 500-pound

bombs, perfect for our troops-in-contact situation.

Just then I saw two puffs of smoke, one red, one white.

Over to fox mike.

"Pappa fox, authenticate golf lima and say your smoke color."

"Pappa foxtrot authenticates november. Red."

"Roger."

The gomers had been listening on the radio and had popped a smoke. They had bet their lives the team's smoke would be white. It was red. They lose.

Over to UHF.

"Catnip, this is Covey 218. There are two smokes on the ground, one white one red. The friendlies are red, I repeat, friendlies are red. Hit the white smoke. Target elevation 4300 feet, wind calm. Cleared in hot from any direction, but do not overfly the red smoke."

"Lead's in from the north."

"Covey 218 holding to the east."

Lead's bombs were right on target.

"Two, you're cleared in hot, same target."

"Two's in from the northwest."

Over to fox mike.

"How do those bombs look, pappa fox?"

"Right on the fucking target! Keep it up. I can hear the chopper inbound."

The chopper had been listening on fox mike and had already identified the friendly position and the LZ. I held in an orbit over the LZ to see if I could identify any threats while they loaded up. No reaction in the LZ area. The chopper took off and headed back to DaNang, with the team safe aboard.

I worked Catnip flight on the area until they were winchester, then sent them home. For the first time in months, I was starting to feel like a FAC again.

30

November 26, 1969

I probably should have felt better about Snake not finding a survivor. That meant that my incompetence as a FAC hadn't had any effect on the rescue of Major Swain, or whoever had put the SAR letter on the jungle floor. The evader who had put the letter there had probably been killed or captured months ago, maybe longer.

But it didn't change the fact that if there had been a survivor, I wouldn't have been any help to him. I had resigned myself to the realization that, although I may have been a pretty good stick-and-rudder pilot, I was a mediocre FAC, at best. Flying FCFs was probably the perfect way for me to finish out my tour.

The previous day, before my afternoon FCF, I received a phone call from a Major at the Judge Advocate General Office. I was required to appear at the court-martial of Airman Davis the next day.

I was flabbergasted. Although Airman Davis didn't have the greatest military bearing and appearance, I couldn't imagine why he would be court-martialed.

It turned out to be for drugs. He had been caught smoking marijuana in the enlisted dormitory, along with several other airmen. It was an open-and-shut case, and he had admitted his guilt. I was being called as a character witness. I liked Davis, and I was glad to do anything I could to help him.

My 1505 uniform was still clean, so I wore it to the court appearance. There were three field-grade officers sitting behind a raised desk, and Airman Davis was with his court-appointed attorney at one table, and the prosecutor was at another. I was sworn in and took my place in the witness box. The defense attorney started.

"Would you please state your name."

"Hamilton Hancock."

"What is your rank?"

"First Lieutenant."

"How do you know the defendant?"

"He works in the Life Support Section of my squadron."

"Have you had any conversations with the

defendant regarding his concern for you?"

"Yes, sir. I had been shot down in August and was reported as missing in action for a couple of days. When I returned to the squadron after my hospital stay, Airman Davis was one of the first people to tell me how happy he was to see me safely back on base."

"Did he mention anything else?"

"He said he had prayed for me the whole time I was missing."

"Thank you. No further questions."

It was time for the prosecutor.

"Your honor, we have no questions of this witness."

That was it. I had told the court that Airman Davis was a decent, religious person. I didn't know if it helped him, or how much. He was sentenced to spend the rest of his Vietnam tour, about six more months, in the Long Binh Jail, referred to as LBJ. Then he would be given a Less-Than-Honorable Discharge. It was better than a Dishonorable Discharge, but only slightly. Maybe instead of smoking dope he would have better off saying he was a conscious objector, like Popeye.

G. E. Nolly

31

November 27, 1969

I went by the BX before my afternoon mission. I almost didn't make it back.

Just as I approached the entrance, I heard automatic weapons fire, and I hit the deck, along with every other GI. M-16 rounds hit the wall where I'd been standing a few seconds earlier, a few feet above where I was now kissing the ground. Then I heard someone yell.

"You man, halt! Drop your weapon!"

I heard more automatic weapons fire from the same location, then what sounded like four or five M-16s firing from another location. Then it was quiet.

Slowly, we all got up and surveyed the situation. A Marine Private lay dead, executed by the MPs. Apparently, he'd gone off the deep end, and started spraying all of us with his M-16. When he didn't drop his weapon, the MPs had no choice but to shoot him.

The war affected the grunts much differently than the way it affected those of us who flew. Other than my run-in with Condom Boy, I wasn't engaged in face-to-face combat, seeing and smelling death up close. I had a sterile experience that was so much less traumatic than what the typical grunt had to deal with. Other than my terror for a total of two days, I had to admit I had it pretty damn good.

My missions, when I had airstrikes, were actually invigorating. After I had gotten over the jitters of initial combat, the missions were almost like the adventure play I used to do as a kid whenever I came home after watching a John Wayne movie. Fish referred to it as "becoming an adrenaline junkie". He might have been right.

For the poor grunts, it was different. It never ended for them. They would go to a village and never know if the gomers would shoot them in the back or welcome them for *nuok mam*. They were told not to pick up crying babies because they might be booby-trapped. And they never got away from it. They watched their buddies get their arms, legs and balls blown off without warning. No wonder some of them went crazy.

One time, there were five of us Coveys who went to the base theater to see *2001: A Space*

Odyssey. Suddenly, an Army Private stood up, held up a grenade, and pulled the pin, holding the handle closed. He started yelling, crazy, unconnected words. We all got up and ran out of the theater through every available exit.

We ran out, the MPs ran in. I don't know how they defused the situation, but there was no explosion, no gunfire. Another GI had succumbed to the horror of close-up war. Lieutenant Royce had told me that kind of thing happened about once a week.

I had been told that half of Vietnam was controlled by the VC – the Viet Cong. Snake said that was probably true.

"Half of each day it's dark. That's when pretty much every Vietnamese is working for the VC. During the day, they work for us. That makes half of Vietnam VC. They're all VC at night, and they're all friendlies during the day."

I used to think he was full of shit. Until today.

The maids who worked in our hooch seemed like they really liked Americans. But I'd had some previous indications that it might all be an act.

A few months earlier, DaNang had come under attack, and the Bully FACs were sent to work fighters on targets right at the base perimeter. They ended up killing 254 gomers, all VC. The next day, our hooch maid was crying hysterically the whole day.

"What's wrong?" I asked.

"My husband die."

"I'm so sorry to hear of your loss. What happened?"

"He have heart attack."

One of the Bully FACs later told me her husband had been killed along the base perimeter, as he was attempting to turn a Claymore mine around. From that time on, I was always suspicious of the Vietnamese who worked on base.

On this day, I was scheduled to fly a late afternoon sortie that had me getting back to base at around 2000 hours, too late to have the Thanksgiving dinner at the chow hall. I was damned lucky.

Several hundred GIs who had eaten at the chow hall became violently ill. Most of them required hospitalization from the dehydration that resulted from extreme diarrhea. Two Gunfighter aircraft never returned from their missions. The pilots of both aircraft had eaten Thanksgiving dinner at the chow hall.

As it turned out, one of the Vietnamese cooks who worked at the chow hall had shit in the dressing. She had done her part for Uncle Ho. One of the other cooks, a *real* friendly, had reported it, but not in time to prevent the dressing from being served. The White Mice, the Vietnamese police, took the maid outside and shot her on the spot.

I had one more order of business to take care of after my mission. I needed to talk to Tom. I went to the MARS station to place a call to Tokyo. After a few rings, Tom answered.

"Hi Tom, it's Ham. Happy Thanksgiving. Over."

"Ham! Happy Thanksgiving to you. It's great to hear from you. But I thought you knew Sam is not here. She's in San Antonio at Officer Training School. Over."

"I know, Tom. I want to talk to you. Over."

G. E. Nolly

32

December 21, 1969

I was scheduled for my Champagne Flight – my final mission – in the morning. Things had been uncharacteristically quiet on the trail for several days, and I wanted to get some target photos for Intel to find out what was going on. Also, I wanted some photos of the AO as a memento of my Vietnam tour.

The O-2 actually had the provision for a belly-mounted KB-18 aerial camera, but we didn't have any KB-18s at DaNang. So, if we wanted to take photos, we relied on hand-held cameras. There were a bunch of beat up old Nikon Fs at the squadron, but they were really heavy and difficult to use with one hand. It was really tough to fly and take pictures at the same time.

Then, about two weeks earlier, we got new cameras, Pentax Spotmatics with motor drives. Each camera had a pistol-grip mount with a trigger to activate the shutter, and the focus was set at "infinity", so there would be no problem with single-hand operation. I was really looking forward to giving them a try. I signed one out on a hand receipt and carried it to the plane.

Task Force Alpha had provided Igloo White information from the seismic sensors that indicated a lot of truck activity along highway 165, near Chavane. I headed directly to the Chavane area to see if I could find anything.

Chavane was an old abandoned grass airfield. Reflectors still lined the edges of the runway, and it almost looked like it could support aircraft operations at any moment. I'd heard that it was an old Japanese airfield from World War II.

There was a dead truck parked out in the open, off to the south side of the east end of the runway. About a year ago, it had been used as a flak trap for unsuspecting FACs, but the word had been out for a long time and nobody paid any attention to it any more. There were no longer active guns, that we knew of, in the area.

I followed highway 165 away from the airfield, and kept my camera on the seat next to me, ready to use if I found anything of interest. I put the highway on the left side of the airplane, and made gentle turns right and left. It was during the left turns that I would be able to see gomer activity, if there was any. The gomers thought we always looked ahead of the airplane, and they would frequently conduct their movements after we passed, thinking we couldn't see them once they were behind the wing.

Sure enough, back at my seven o'clock, I saw a truck cross the road, from the cover of the jungle on one side of the road to the cover of the jungle on the other side. I kept my eyes on the exact location and began a steeper turn back toward that area.

I picked out a distinctive landmark, a small bend in the road, and then looked further away to see if there were any other landmarks that could point my eyes back to the target. I used the runway at Chavane for a yardstick. The target was exactly one runway length north of the east end of the runway. The bend in the road sort of pointed to the target. Okay, now I could leave the immediate target area and find my way back.

I flew off to the east and set up an orbit over an area a few klicks away, to make the gomers think I was interested in something else. I turned on the gyro-stabilized binoculars, locked onto the target area, and zoomed in to the highest setting.

Sure enough, I saw some vehicle tracks in the dirt alongside the road that indicated truck activity. I was pretty sure there was a truck park there, I just couldn't determine which side of the road it was on. I flew back to the target area and made a wide sweeping circle, taking pictures from every angle. If I couldn't get any air assets, I would at least have photos to give to Intel.

I switched my transmitter over to VHF and called Hillsboro.

"Hillsboro, Covey 218, vicinity Delta 33. I have a truck park and need air."

"Roger, Covey 218, we're sending Sharkbait 41 to you, flight of two fox fours, CBU-24s and mark-82s. ETA 10 minutes. Strike frequency Echo."

"Roger, thank you."

I looked forward to working with Sharkbait Flight. Sharkbait was the call sign of the F-4s from Cam Ranh Air Base. When I was at the Cam Ranh hospital, I went by the F-4 squadron a few times, just to visit with the jocks. I got to know a few of them, and they showed me around one of the airplanes in the maintenance hangar. Sitting in the cockpit convinced me that I really ought to request an F-4 for my follow-on assignment. That really worked out well!

I switched my UHF to strike frequency Echo and waited. After a few minutes, the F-4s arrived at the rendezvous.

"Sharkbait, check."

"Two."

"Hello, Covey 218, Sharkbait 41, flight of two fox fours at the rendezvous point. Mark-82s and CBU-24s. Angels twenty-two. Twenty minutes playtime."

"Roger Sharkbait. Look due south, at angels seven. I'm giving you a wing flash now."

I rocked my wings several times and performed a quick aileron roll. The O-2 wasn't really an acrobatic aircraft, but an aileron roll wasn't all that much different than the maneuver we needed to perform a rocket pass. And I wanted to get my rocks off one last time.

"We have you in sight, Covey."

"Roger, the target area is off my left wing. Truck park. Negative reaction so far. I'm in for the mark."

I rolled into a 120-degree bank to the left and pulled the nose of my aircraft through into a 30-degree dive. When the pipper in my gun sight tracked up to the target, I fired off a willie pete. I pulled off hard to the right, then banked left to see where my mark hit. It was a perfect mark, right on the road adjacent to my target.

"Sharkbait has your mark in sight."

"Okay, Sharkbait, the target is a truck park on both sides of the road, alongside my mark. I want you to run in with mark-82s from north to south, with a break to the west. Lead, put your bombs in the trees next to my mark. Either side of the road. Two, I want you to take the other side of the road. I'll be holding off to the east."

"Sharkbait lead is in."

Sharkbait lead put his bombs exactly where I wanted, and we immediately got huge secondary explosions. As lead pulled off target, there was heavy fire at his aircraft from a ZSU 23-4, located about a klick to the west of the target.

I transmitted, "Number two, hold high and dry. I want to put you in on that gun. Do you have the location, or do you want me to mark?"

Before number two could answer, lead came back on the radio.

"Sharkbait lead's been hit."

I immediately got on the radio again, "Lead, head south, I repeat, head south. Number two, hold high and dry."

Sharkbait two acknowledged.

"Roger."

Sharkbait lead had apparently heard me, he was heading south. I could see flames trailing from lead's aircraft, and they were moving forward, gradually engulfing the entire aircraft.

I was fairly sure lead knew he was on fire, but I didn't want to take any chances. "Sharkbait lead, you're on fire!"

Now burning pieces were separating from lead's aircraft.

Lead came on the radio one last time.

"Sharkbait lead bailing out."

33

December 21, 1969

Sharkbait lead's aircraft was in a slight bank to the right, at about 5000 feet. The rear canopy separated, followed immediately by the ejection of the rear seat pilot. About a half-second later, the front canopy separated and the front seat pilot ejected.

I was able to keep both ejection seats in sight, and watched in horror as the back seat pilot separated from his seat, his parachute automatically deployed, and the parachute didn't open – it was a streamer. He plummeted down into the jungle. There was no beeper.

I looked at the front pilot's seat and watched him separate. As his chute opened, I heard his high-to-low-sweep beeper on Guard. The front-seater had a good chute. I set up an orbit to the east and watched him descend, as I selected VHF and called Hillsboro.

"Mayday, mayday, mayday. Hillsboro, this is

Covey 218, we have Sharkbait lead down in the area of Delta 33. Need immediate SAR."

"Roger, Covey 218, we are notifying King."

I switched back to UHF.

"Sharkbait two, say playtime remaining."

"I can give you 30 minutes, then I need to RTB. Listen, Covey, we need to get a SAR for lead."

"I'm working on it."

"I mean," he responded, "we *really* need to get lead picked up."

"Roger, hold high and dry off to the east, over me. Climb to your best endurance altitude and let me know your angels when you get there. Left hand orbit. We're going to need to use you to go after that gun when SAR gets here."

"Roger."

I watched the front-seat pilot descend to the ground. He landed in an open meadow. At least he wasn't hung up in the trees. I saw him release from his parachute harness and head south to find cover. Right after he disappeared into the tree line, the beeper went silent and he came up on Guard, using his survival radio.

"This is Sharkbait 41 Alpha. I'm on the move heading south. Unhurt."

I saw about twenty gomers entering the meadow from the north. I went to Guard frequency.

"Sharkbait 41 Alpha, Covey 218, you need to keep moving. There are gomers north of you heading to where you came down."

"Roger."

Back to strike frequency Echo.

"Sharkbait 42, Covey 218. I need to put you in with your CBU on the meadow. I'm in for the mark."

"Roger."

I rolled in and put a willie pete dead center in the meadow. The gomers had flooded in and were now everywhere.

"Hit my mark. Cleared in hot with one CBU from any direction. I'll be off to the east."

"Two's in."

I watched Sharkbait 42 release his CBU, saw the spark that indicated the canister opened, then saw the donut-shaped sparkling pattern, right on target. I put the gyro-stabilized binoculars on the target area and saw a bunch of dead bodies. But I saw some gomers still moving through the meadow, headed south. And more were entering the meadow.

"Okay two, I need you to keep making passes

on that target until you're winchester CBU."

"Two's in."

Sharkbait 42 made three more passes on the meadow, all right on target. There were a bunch of dead gomers. But there were still more coming in from the north.

Just then the ZSU 23-4 opened up again, this time targeting me. I jinked out of the way without too much trouble. I was getting good at dodge gball.

If I had to, I'd put Sharkbait 42 in on the gun now, but I wanted to reserve his mark-82s for the SAR. I went over to VHF.

"Hillsboro, Covey 218, what's the status of the SAR?"

"Covey 218, Jolly 22 is departing NKP now with Spad 11 Flight. ETA 30 minutes."

"Roger, I need more air for the cap right now. I don't care what ordnance. I want them ASAP."

"We're scrambling Dingus Flight from Ubon. They should be there in fifteen to twenty minutes."

Shit. It looked like the gomers would be on top of Alpha before my air arrived.

Over to Guard.

"Four-one Alpha, say your position."

"I'm still moving south. I hear automatic weapons fire coming from where I landed. I'm at the edge of a tree line now, alongside what looks like an old grass strip."

"Okay Alpha, Covey 218. Cross the strip and hide in the tree line on the other side, the south side."

"Roger."

Strike Frequency Echo.

"Sharkbait 42, I need to put your mark-82s on the tree line, north side of the midfield of that grass strip. Do you have the strip in sight?"

"Affirmative."

"Okay, hold high and dry until I call you in. Be ready to roll in on short notice."

"Roger."

I checked out the tree line on the north side of the runway. No gomers yet. I kept checking, and after a few minutes the gomers appeared. I could see flashes. They were firing at Alpha.

"Sharkbait 42 roll in now, parallel to the runway, in the tree line, midfield, north side. North side only."

"Two's in."

His bombs were right on target. He held for

a few more minutes, then made another run. And another.

"Sharkbait two is winchester."

"Any chance you have twenty mike-mike?" I was hoping he had a cannon, but I already knew what the answer would be.

"Negative. Sharkbait 42 is bingo."

"Roger, Sharkbait, cleared RTB. I'll pass BDA over the landline."

Back to VHF.

"Hillsboro, I need those fighters and SAR, NOW"

There was a short pause. My guess was that Hillsboro was contacting Jolly and Dingus.

"Ten more minutes."

Fuck! We didn't have ten minutes. The gomers were everywhere in the north tree line, muzzle flashes everywhere. I still had 12 willie petes left. Time to become an attack aircraft.

I rolled in on a rocket pass down the runway, angling in slightly toward the north. I fired off one willie pete at a time, and made 12 passes.

I was now a war criminal.

34

December 21, 1969

The Geneva Convention prohibited the use of white phosphorous weapons. The willie pete rocket explodes with the lethal radius of a hand grenade, and the phosphorous sticks to the skin and burns at a temperature of five thousand degrees. It's terrible. It's illegal.

So is skinning a helpless captive. Or shooting at someone descending in a parachute. Or setting up a flak trap. Or shooting rockets at helpless South Vietnamese civilians.

And besides, we were fighting a fucking war in Laos, where our government didn't even acknowledge our presence. Every fucking mission got logged as "South Vietnam". We weren't even there, so the Geneva Convention wouldn't apply. And if it did, I didn't give a fuck. I wasn't going to let those bastards get Alpha.

I was out of willie petes, and SAR was still eight or nine minutes away.

Over to Guard.

"How are you doing, Alpha?"

"The gomers have me pinned down on the south side of the runway. They're shooting at me from across the runway and also from somewhere south of me."

I had to do something. I climbed to 5000 feet and feathered my rear prop. Then I released my lap belt and moved to the passenger seat, opened the passenger door, and pulled the red door release handle. With the rear prop feathered, I didn't need to worry about the door hitting the rear prop as I jettisoned it. As soon as the door was gone, I unfeathered the rear prop, and the engine started right up.

I opened the karabiner that attached my AR-15 to my survival vest, put the rifle in full auto, and pushed the throttles to the firewall to fly down the runway at max airspeed. I went down to about five feet, screaming down the runway, firing my AR-15 out the open door at the north tree line. I emptied the 20-round clip in about a second. Shit! I should have used short bursts.

I pulled up into a chandelle, put another

magazine in the AR-15, and made another run,. This time I was shooting out the left window. It was a smaller opening to shoot through, but it would have to do. Ejected shell casings hammered against the instrument panel. The glass on the Vertical Speed Indicator cracked. I didn't care.

Over to VHF.

"Status on the SAR."

"Five more minutes."

"We don't have five fucking minutes!"

If I didn't get Alpha out of there right now, there would be no use having a SAR.

Over to Guard.

"Alpha, how high is the grass on the runway?"

"Not very high. Maybe eight, ten inches."

"Okay, get ready to go for an airplane ride."

I jettisoned my rocket pods and dove for the ground. I needed to get as low as I could as I approached the runway, so they wouldn't see me coming. I unsynchronized my propellers, so that the engines would make a beat frequency sound, making it more difficult to determine my location by ear.

I came in from the west. As I crossed over

the end of the strip, I put down the landing gear and pulled the throttles to idle. I touched down a third of the way down the runway, and rapidly slowed to a crawl right at midfield. I suppose the gomers were totally surprised, because there was no ground fire. None. Alpha came running from the tree line and leaped through the open door into the passenger seat while the plane was still moving.

I firewalled the throttles and hoped I still knew how to perform a soft-field takeoff. I got airborne and stayed in ground effect, trying to accelerate.

The gomers quickly caught on to what I was doing, and opened up from the tree lines, both left and right, with massive automatic weapons fire. I could hear our aircraft taking a few hits, but it was still flying. I think the gomers hadn't gotten the hang of leading a moving target. They'd probably never gone quail hunting.

I handed the AR-15 to Alpha and tried to tell him to kill those bastards. The sound of the engines, the open door, and the ground fire drowned out what I was saying, but he caught on and started shooting out the door. I could see gomers firing back, and some were falling down as he fired.

I climbed up to 5000 feet and tried to figure

out which way to head. The front engine was starting to run rough, and my fuel gauges showed a huge discrepancy between the left and right tanks. I must have taken a hit in the right wing. I headed toward Lima 44, about 50 miles due west.

I still had work to do. I didn't want the SAR forces coming anywhere near that ZSU 23-4. I got on VHF.

"Hillsboro, cancel the SAR. Keep the SAR airplanes away from Delta 33. There's an active 23 mike-mike in the area. I have Sharkbait 41 Alpha in my aircraft. We've taken numerous hits, and we're recovering at Lima 44. Send Jolly 22 to Lima 44 for our pickup."

"Roger. We'll pass the info."

The front engine quit about two miles on final approach to Lima 44. Now I would need to pump the gear down, since the hydraulic pump was on the front engine. I feathered the front prop, put down the gear handle, reached down, extended the manual hydraulic pump handle, and started pumping. Then it occurred to me: I had a helper. I made a pumping motion with my right hand.

"Here. Pump this," I said. He probably didn't hear me, but he figured out what to do.

The gear came down about a half-mile on final, and we had an uneventful landing. I followed a beat-up follow-me truck, probably the same one as last time, and shut down the airplane. When we got out, Alpha gave me a big hug. He didn't want to release me, and he was shaking.

I knew how he felt. I hugged him back, and then we both started crying.

"I, I don't know how to thank you. I'm Herb McCall."

"I'm Hamfist Hancock. No problem, Herb. I've been in your situation, and I understand completely."

Just like last time, Jolly 22 landed in the parking spot next to our airplane. I reached into my plane and grabbed the AR-15 and the Pentax, and then we climbed aboard the chopper. I went up to the cockpit and saw Vince.

"Hey, Vince, we've got to stop meeting this way! I'm on my Champagne Flight"

"You got that right, Hamfist. So am I."

Alpha took off his survival vest and guzzled down the water the PJ handed to him. When his vest was off, I saw the rank insignia on his shoulders. Alpha was a Brigadier General!

35

December 21, 1969

As we approached NKP, Vince motioned for me to come forward to the cockpit.

"I got a call from my Operations Center. They said for you to stand by on the ramp, there's a Major Scoville on his way to NKP in an OV-10 to fly you back to DaNang."

"Got it."

That made sense. I needed a way to get back to DaNang, and I suspected Scooter couldn't wait to get me onto the freedom bird out of Vietnam and out of his hair.

About two hours after I arrived at NKP, Scooter arrived in his OV-10. He had an extra parachute harness for me, and gave me a quick seat check-out. I had already flown a few flights in the back seat of an OV-10, so I didn't need much instruction. The most important part of the check-out was the refresher training in how to use the ejection seat. The upper and lower ejection handles were totally different from the ejection handles in the T-37 and T-38, the only other ejection-seat-equipped aircraft I had flown previously.

"You're sure you know how to eject if we need to?" Scooter asked.

"Yes, sir. Either upper face curtain or lower handles, right?"

"Right."

I put the camera and AR-15 in the cargo bay, along with my back-pack parachute, and strapped into the back seat of Scooter's OV.

We had an uneventful flight back to DaNang, and there was a large squadron arrival party waiting for us when we landed. A fire truck hosed me down after I deplaned, and then we piled into the Covey truck, the new replacement for Balser's jeep, and drove to the Doom Club.

I marched into the club one last time, wearing my hat, walked up to the large bell over the bar, rang it, and yelled "Dead bug!". And, one last time, I just stood there, grinning, while everyone else rushed to get on their backs with their arms waving in the air.

I made an extra effort to not get totally shit-faced drunk, so I wouldn't black out this time. I wanted to remember this moment, and I managed to stay semi-sober.

It was a really nice going-away party. The guys presented me with a goodbye gift, a pair of jockey shorts with a horseshoe-shaped magnet sewn over the left ass cheek. I put them on over my flight suit and paraded around, while everyone chanted, "Magnet ass, magnet ass!" On second thought, maybe I wasn't as semi-sober as I had thought.

Then it was time to start singing. We all sang a bunch of combat-related songs we had written. I wrote a short song, and sang it on the fly. In the spirit of the season, I chose a song with a Christmas motif.

I composed as I sang, to the tune of "Oh Little Town of Bethlehem".

Oh little town of old Chavane
Wherein an airfield lies,
Just one dead truck
But what the fuck,
The guns light up the skies.

36

December 25, 1969

The previous several days had been very strange. I didn't have anything to do, other than pack up my few belongings and ship them out to Mather Air Force Base through the Traffic Management Office. I put the rest of my things in an A3 bag and put my nice civvies in a hang-up bag I had bought at the BX.

I wandered around the base and took some last-minute photos, and tried to get photos of my friends at the squadron. It was an empty feeling, watching my comrades take off on missions and knowing I was now just an observer.

I had a very early morning flight on one of the R&R birds to Tokyo. Right after I returned from Cam Ranh, I had requested two weeks of leave in Tokyo at the end of my tour, and it was immediately approved. I found it hard to believe it had already been five months since I had been on this same flight for R&R.

When I arrived at Yokota Air Base, at about 0700, I took the train to downtown Tokyo. I knew Tom would send a limo for me if I asked, but I wanted to already be in town when I called.

I had made a room reservation at the Sanno, the downtown officers' recreation facility, several weeks earlier, and I wanted to be changed into my good civvies when I met up with Tom, Miyako and, especially, Sam.

There was a young Second Lieutenant, Frank, who was on his R&R break, who also planned to go to the Sanno. He'd never been to Japan before, and I took him under my wing. With an entire five days of experience, I was the old head in getting around.

We caught a cab from the Passenger Terminal to the Fussa train station, and I showed Frank how to use the ticket machine and how to interpret the diagram that showed what track we should take. I was pretty proud of myself.

"We need to go to Akasaka-Mitsuke," I said, pointing to the map. "The Sanno is just a few blocks from the station."

We got on the train, and I decided to teach

Frank the few Japanese words I had learned from Sam.

"To say 'Good Morning' you say *Ohayo*. It sounds just like the state, Ohio."

"*Ohayo*," he repeated. The commuters on the train smiled.

I proceeded to teach him all the other standard words and phrases I knew. I ended with an explanation of how to express hunger.

"Instead of saying 'I am hungry', you actually say 'My stomach has become empty'. So you say *Sakana-ga sukimashita*."

"*Sakana-ga sukimashita*," he repeated.

Again, the commuters smiled politely. I was really proud of how much I had learned.

We arrived at the Sanno at about 0830, and I called Sam as soon as I got settled in my room. She answered on the second ring.

"Merry Christmas, Captain!" I said.

"Ham! I've been waiting to hear from you. Where are you?"

"I'm at the Sanno, room 305."

"I'll be there in about a half-hour. My dad wants to speak to you."

"Okay. I'll be waiting for you. Bye bye, honey."

"Bye bye. Here's Daddy."

"Ham, I'm so glad you got here safely. I know you want to be alone with Sam, but can we plan to have dinner together, the four of us?"

"Absolutely, Tom. Tell Sam how we're going to dress, and we'll see you around seven."

"Okay. See you then."

I shaved and changed into my good civvies, the suit Tom had made for me. I really wanted to look good for Sam.

After what seemed like an eternity, there was a knock at the door. I opened it and Sam rushed into my arms. It was so good to hold her again!

We shared a long embrace and a passionate kiss, and then we pulled apart to look at each other.

"You've lost more weight," she said.

"And you've cut your hair," I answered.

It hadn't occurred to me until just then that she would have had to cut her beautiful, long hair when she entered Officer Training School. Long hair or short, she looked absolutely gorgeous.

Naturally, we made love. Not hurried, frantic love. Slow, passionate love.

Afterward, we showered and dressed. I was hungry. Really hungry.

"*Sakana-ga sukimashita*," I said, proudly.

"What did you say," Sam replied, holding her hand over her mouth as she giggled.

"*Sakana-ga sukimashita*," I repeated. "I'm hungry."

Now Sam was really laughing.

"You just said your fish has become empty! *Sakana* is fish. *Onaka* is stomach."

"Oh, that's right. *Onaka-ga sukimashita*."

Sakana, *onaka*, they sounded a lot alike. Then I remembered the polite smiles on the train as I had repeatedly instructed Frank how to say that his fish had become empty!

We went to the casual restaurant for breakfast, and sat in a quiet corner.

"I have something to show you," Sam said, as she reached into her purse. She pulled out an envelope containing photos, and handed it to me.

I removed the photos from the envelope and looked through them. The first photo was a picture of Sam in her new Air Force Captain uniform, receiving the Distinguished Graduate Award at Officer Training School. She looked fantastic.

"You made DG! Congratulations!" I said, giving her a warm hug.

The next photo was of Sam in her uniform, sitting behind a desk at her new assignment, in the Judge Advocate General Office at Yokota.

I flipped through the photos, and then did a double-take. I saw photos of Sam with my mother, at my house, and at the beach.

"I, I'm confused," I said, "When …"

"You got to meet my parents, so I thought it was only fair for me to meet your mother. So after OTS I flew to Mobile, rented a car and drove to Pensacola. Your mom's really nice. She even let me stay in your room."

"You stayed in my room?"

"Yeah. I even helped your mom clean out your closet. We got fifty dollars for all those old Playboy magazines you'd been collecting. A dollar a piece. It paid for our dinner at the Chart House."

"I'm glad somebody got some use out of them. I don't think I need them anymore."

"I suppose you're going to tell me you only read the articles."

"Actually, I only looked at the pictures."

"Here, look at this." She shuffled through the photos until she found the one she was looking for. "We went to Fort Walton Beach. The sand is so white, and it squeaks when you walk on it!"

"I know. I grew up in that area. I'm so glad you met my mom. I bet she's crazy about you."

"We got along great. I told her about visiting you in Cam Ranh Bay. And I told her how much I love you."

"I'm sure she's going to love you as much as I do." I paused for a moment, then said, "Can you show me how to take the train to Shibuya? I really want to go there with you."

"Sure. Let's go."

We took the train, and stepped out of the station at the entrance next to the statue of Hachiko. Like before, there was crowd around the statue. I looked across the street at the coffee shop where we had sat some five months earlier.

"Let's go back up there. I want to be able to talk to you in a more private place."

"Okay."

We entered the coffee shop, went upstairs, and took the table next to the window, the same table where we had sat last time.

"Last night I got a call from General McCall. He was the survivor I helped rescue a couple of

229

days ago."

"I didn't know you helped rescue a general."

"I didn't know it either, at the time. It was a tough SAR, and there were a lot of people involved. The general probably called everyone who helped."

"Anyway," I continued, "he told me he wanted to help me with my assignment. He had heard about how I had been promised my choice of assignments when I volunteered for Vietnam. And how the Air Force went back on that promise."

"So he said he can get you a fighter?"

"He said he can get me any assignment I want."

"Ham, that's wonderful! So, what kind of assignment did you ask him for? An F-4? An F-100? What? And where?"

I thought back to my Thanksgiving call to Tom.

"Tom. I want to talk to you. Over."

"Is something wrong? Over."

"Not at all. Tom, the reason I'm calling is I'd like permission to ask for Samantha's hand in marriage. Over."

"Ham, you're the son I never had. I'd be

thrilled if you and Samantha were to get married. I'm honored to give you my blessing, with three conditions. Over."

Cheers erupted from the MARS waiting room.

"Anything, Tom. Over."

"First, I want you to be engaged for at least a year before you get married. I want you to know each other through all four seasons. Second, I want you to go to pre-marital counseling. Smooth out the rough edges that all relationships have. Finally, I want to provide the diamond. Over."

Again, cheers from the waiting room.

"Tom, I'm happy to comply. But, when it comes to the ring, at least let me pay you for it, a little every month. I'll be a Captain in about a year, and I'll be able to afford it. I want to pay for the ring, Tom, but I'd like your help picking out a great diamond. Over."

"You have a deal, Ham. And, by the way, you're lucky Sam's not still a Japanese citizen. Over."

"Why is that? Over."

"Japanese tradition is for the groom to pay for the wedding. I love you, son. Goodbye. Over."

Now Sam was looking at me, expectantly.

"Well, what assignment did you get?"

"Sam, I got the assignment that will give me everything I ever dreamed of."

"Come on. Tell me!"

"I got a T-39 to Yokota Air Base."

Sam looked shocked.

"I, I don't understand. You had your heart set on getting a fighter."

I looked into Sam's eyes as I got down on one knee and reached into my pocket and took out the ring.

"Sam, when I was on the jungle floor I did a lot of soul searching, and I realized what is really important to me. Someday, if it's meant to be, I may fly a fighter. But what I really want right now is to be with you, every day. I lost my chance with you once. I don't want that to happen again. I first fell in love with you right here. I love you with all my heart, and I want to spend the rest of my life with you. Will you marry me?"

Sam had brought her hands up to her face, covering her mouth. She lowered her hands and slipped her finger into the ring.

"Yes. Yes!"

I stood up, planted a passionate kiss on her lips, and hugged her tightly. Then I reached into my other pocket and withdrew my paint bottle, my miniature brush and my *daruma*.

"Now I'd like you to help me with something," I said.

"Anything. What?"

"I want you to help me paint the other eye."

G. E. Nolly

The adventure continues . . .

Follow the adventures of Hamfist Hancock here at:

www.GENolly.com

www.HamfistAdventures.com

Stay in touch with the author via:

Twitter: http://twitter.com/gnolly

If you liked *Hamfist Down!,* please post a review on Amazon.

And stand by for *Hamfist Over Hanoi,* coming soon.

Other books by G.E.Nolly:

Hamfist Over The Trail

This Is Your Captain Speaking: Insider Air Travel Secrets

This Is Your Captain Speaking: Layover Security For Road Warriors

ABOUT THE AUTHOR

George Nolly served as a pilot in the United States Air Force, flying 315 combat missions on two successive tours of duty in Vietnam, flying O-2A and F-4 aircraft. In 1983, George received Tactical Air Command Instructor of the Year Award for his service as an instructor in the Air Force Forward Air Controller course.

Following his Air Force duty, he hired on with United Airlines and rose to the position of B-777 Check Captain. He also served as a Federal Flight Deck Officer. Following his retirement from United, George accepted a position as a B-777 Captain with Jet airways, operating throughout Europe, Asia and the Middle East.

In 2000, George was selected as a Champion in the Body-for-LIFE Transformation Challenge, and is a Certified Fitness Trainer and self-defense expert with more than 30 years' experience in combative arts.

George received a Bachelor of Science Degree from the United States Air Force Academy and received a Master of Science Degree, in Systems Management, from the University of Southern California. He completed all of the required studies for a second Master of Science Degree, in Education, at the University of Southern California, and received his Doctor of Business Administration Degree, specializing in Homeland Security, from Northcentral University.

He now flight instructs in the B777 and B787.

CPSIA information can be obtained at www.ICGtesting.com
Printed in the USA
LVOW131934280513

335806LV00001B/11/P